ACKNOWLEDGEMENTS

To the cosplay women that fueled my fantasies and have now reaffirmed to me that, yes, I do indeed want to fuck a woman dressed as a superhero before I die.

For my youth that, without you, I would never know comic books or the reasoning behind them and that they actually serve a purpose in life.

To the superhero in us all, who strives to get out everyday and punch a motherfucker out and save the day!

For Leo and Tracey, who re-ignited my faith that married people are secretly still pervs.

Other Books by Riley S. Brown:

<u>The Chronicles of Ar Solon Series:</u>

Book 17: In the Care of Kobolds (TBA)

Book 18: Chains of Solace (TBA)

Book 19: Forgotten Angel (Released April 2010)

Book 20: The Paths We All Walk: A Collection of Tales (TBA)

Book 21: The Healer, Part I (Released August 2011)

Book 21: The Healer, Part II (Winter 2014)

Writing under the alias Titus Strong:

<u>A Man's Romance Novel Series:</u>

The Temptress: Book One (August 2011)

A Corporate Feeling: Book Two

How Santa Ate My Cookies and Other Festive Tales of Erotic Fiction: Christmas Special (Released August 2014)

<u>A Young Gentleman's Romance Novel Series:</u>

The Pill **(Released October 2014)**

The Pill: Second Dose

The Pill: Possible Solutions

<u>Available for purchase at:</u>

www.bandn.com and www.amazon.com

The Pill

BY

TITUS STRONG

"If anyone knows what it's like to be on the outside, I do. Sometimes I feel like I'm out there fighting all alone. Sometimes I feel like giving up. But, then I remember that what I stand for is more important than anything else."

- SUPERMAN

PRELUDE

With all the erotic fiction coming out lately for the ladies, I felt it quite sad that men didn't get the same attention. So, without further ado, I offer you porn! Yes, porn of your own caliber, gentlemen; aesthetically pleasing yet altogether different from what women see as exciting and enthralling. I've written a couple of books of erotic fiction so far and, I think it's safe to say this; those books were written with men and women readers in mind.
This one, however, is just for you, gentlemen.

I couldn't just give you some cock and pussy action without putting something of use within the story, now could I? What would be the fun in that? As a writer, I like to push my boundaries and I also enjoy cross-genre work. So, I thought to myself, "What better way to do this by telling of a coming-of-age story with a twist?"

But now, I can't help myself. The nerd in me wants to come out and I can't (and won't) stop it. I've been oversaturated with superhero movies and the media following them in the past few years and feel that it is only necessary that I put my two cents in when it comes to superheroes. Yes, us men are fantasizing while at work of flying and spinning webs as we hurl ourselves through the city streets, saving some damsel in distress. Of course, with this, comes the dilemma.

What/Who would you do with yours?

I spent years, years ladies and gentleman, talking about what superhero power I would want to have. I know that every young man, at some point or another, played that game with their friends. "What superhero power, if you could have any in the world, would you want to have?" For me, I played around with the idea of teleporting like good old Nightcrawler or flying like Supes. Everyone chooses flying. Of course, unless you are of the 90s and 2000's generation and have a hard-on for adamantium claws. Who doesn't love the rough-and-tumble drifter with muttonchops and half a stogie shoved into the corner of his mouth? All of that screams the Marlboro Man come to life. And you know how much chics dig the Marlboro Man, right?

But no one, I repeat NO ONE that I know has ever asked to be desirable to those that they are attracted to themselves. Because, I'm sure at some point, no one thought that was a power. Read on, my fellow lusty Power Girl fans, read on, my fans of a vigilante dressed in skin-tight leather serving justice, read on, any one who's gone to comic conventions and died at the veritable amount of flesh they could look at but not touch. I am here to free you from the oppression that is comic envy!

Titus Strong

Trying to be a hero to the nerds

July 22, 2012

Prologue:
Origins of an Artist

April 9th, 2007.

Many people can pick out specific dates and times in their lives when things changed; when they either took a turn for the worse or the better. It could be something as simple as breaking up with that girl that never appreciated you, learning the final notes to Moonlight Sonata on piano, or keeping one of your promises to yourself, you know, one of those that you made back during New Year's Even when you were three sheets to the wind and full of yourself?

'I'm going to change the world,' your drunken ass would say and, while you were drunk, you would really believe what you were talking about as if you were going to do it. But then, the next day would come rearing its ugly head and you would put it off from one day to the next until you're back at square one, another year gone by, nothing really done with your life, nothing made better, nothing changed.

This is not one of those stories. This story is about change, but in a more grueling, much more painful sort. And the time in my life is when I realized that my father was never coming back. He had been in my life for nearly 12 years and then he just walked away, never looking back.

But he left me something in the process. Deep in the crevasses of our attic, amidst the items that mom and I were trying out best to get rid of before the bank seized the house, I found it; my destiny. Little did I know that my destiny would be wrapped tightly in nearly air tight plastic and contain a backboard, a few colored pages that aged well with time and consisted of a story, a few square panels, and a colorful protagonist defending the innocent against tyranny, oppression, etc. Little did I know that my life would not only change with the introduction of comics into my life, but I would find my destiny within them. And it all happened on April 9th, 2007.'

*   *   *

"Mom, I think that's most of the boxes." Tobias hefted the last of the boxes marked Christmas decorations down to his mom, Deborah, his mother dusting each box off before taping them up tight and writing on each of them with a black sharpie.

"That's fine, honey. Grab the rest of what's up there and we'll go through them down here. I'll order some lunch while we do it. We need to get the rest of these boxes on the truck. We have until tonight to load up anything we want to keep before the bank comes tomorrow."

But Tobias didn't need another reminder about the loss of their home to the bank. The red notices posted on their door when they weren't at home, the incessant calls throughout the day and the harassing voicemails left on the answering machine were enough. And, if Tobias ever felt like it wasn't enough, he could always look at the stack of paperwork that was left at their doorstep by the mailman and the creases across his mother's forehead when she looked at the mail all those nights when she thought her son was sleeping and not peeking around the corner into the living room.

The cancer had taken a toll on the entire family. First, it was just a 'simple' procedure, his mom going to the hospital to get something strange looked at. The word lump took on a whole new meaning to her son after she came back with the results from the lab. She had breast cancer.

For Tobias Merchon, that meant the family had it along with her. But, for his father, he wouldn't last long. After the first chemotherapy session, Weston never came home from work one day. Word got around that he had stayed with his sister and, a few weeks later, divorce paperwork arrived at their soon to be foreclosed home. The ties had been severed. Tobias was left to fend for his mother while the cancer ate away at her very insides, leaving her weak and frail for months at a time.

So many times, Tobias had lain awake by her bedside at the hospital and kept watch, making sure she was comfortable, though her ragged breathing and circles under her eyes showed that the "alright" that she told him was just a lie to keep her son safe and not completely damaged from the cancer as well.

But on to destiny.

With breast cancer battled and nearly conquered, a divorce in the past, a move was their present and their future was unknown, Tobias back to as good as his spirits would allow him to be. His mother was back with him, for now at least.

The bank wanted everything. Debbie's car was suddenly gone, the one that she had worked so hard for. Much of what his mother had earned for her 401k had to be cashed in and used to pay off the lawyers to keep the banks away from her savings. The banks gave a 30-day notice to vacate the home before it was seized, which left a single parent and her son to find a relatively small place to get based on the savings that Deborah had in the bank for a rainy day.

They moved on, against the currents; but together, determined.

"There's just a few more boxes and then I'll be down. Extra pepperoni, okay?"

There was no response downstairs.

"Mom? Mom, you okay?" Tobias felt his heard skip a beat. Then he heard something.

"Yes, I'd like to place an order. Delivery. 6 Arbutus Way." His mother's voice trailed off. The 13-year-old breathed a sigh of relief.

Tobias was famished, he just realized.

Famished and covered in sweat and dust. Great combination!

He kept the work gloves on for the last three boxes in the corner of the attic, the afternoon April heat in Illinois apparent in the stuffy, enclosed space.

"I got you the extra pepperoni, Tobias."

"Thanks."

He reached for the box in front of him and grabbed underneath the edges with his fingers, lifting with his knees. It looked like a heavy box just from what he had already been hefting, so he prepared for the worst.

Probably some old fine china. Yeah, something breakable all stacked together so I can get blamed for it when it comes crashing down.

Tobias was not a strong young man at all. He was thin and somewhat frail, which left him prone to bullying and teasing from the kids in his 9th grade gym class. But he could run. He could run well. Nevertheless, it didn't help him prepare for moving boxes, especially ones that didn't have the bottom of them taped closed properly.

All the contents of the box came crashing down onto the floor when he lifted it up off the floor.

"Dammit! How did I know that was going to happen?"

He stood holding the box for a few seconds more before discarding it among the rubbish they weren't taking with them still up in the attic.

"I'm going to have to get another box. And tape it up this time! Good!" Then he looked down at what had spilled out around his feet.

All of the faces of heroes stared up at him. For a time, it took Tobias a moment to recognize them as comic books. But, as he caught the shape of the bagged and boarded items, a slight glare hitting them from one of the attic windows, he noticed the famous superheroes that frequented many of the cartoon channels in the morning. Superman, Hulk, Shazam, Wolverine, Batman, Wonder Woman and a plethora of other characters he didn't even know the names or faces of until he glanced upon them lay on the floor, the comics almost looking as if they were waiting for his next move.

These must've been my dads.

"Mom? Did dad collect comics?"

It took her a second to respond.

"Yeah, he had quite a collection. Why, did you find them?"

Tobias grabbed up a nearby empty box and doubled up on the tape at the bottom. He began putting them into the box.

Yes, mom. Yes, I did.

It didn't take long for Tobias to become a useful young man for the single parent family he now belonged to. He had seen a comic book store before and some of the comics he remembered buying with his dad at a comic store years ago came flooding into his mind, several covers still burned into his mind when his father had picked them out from the myriad of others that had been on the shelf. Tobias' purpose was simple; to sell what he could from the old house to make a future for him and his mother.

And the comics were one of the first things to go.

20

That afternoon, after the pizza was eaten and the leftovers were placed in the fridge for later, Tobias and his mother Deborah drove him to the comic book store.

Little did Tobias know that what he held was a treasure trove full of comics worth a pretty penny- as well as the first look at what his destiny would hold.

Episode One:

Not Much Has Changed

"Oh fuck, baby! That feels so good! Don't stop!" Maggie's slippery ass bounced against his thighs, his cock slamming deeper and deeper into her, her trembling hands grabbing at the edge of the sofa for a hold.

The living room was completely empty except for Maggie and Douglas taking advantage of his parents being out of town for a convention. He drilled his latest piece, both of them dripping in sweat in just a few minutes time, Maggie not really knowing what she had gotten herself into until it was too late.

You see, Douglas Winterman was the older brother of Mark and assistant manager to Fan-Dome Comics and Collectibles in Bolingbrook, Illinois. He had been there since he was a teenager but, somehow, never followed the passion for comics that his father and younger brother had. Instead, well, he liked other things.

"Take it, you dirty little girl! Take it!"

He grabbed a handful of her dark hair and continued to drill her from behind. He was built, he had stamina, he was attractive and had a nice car; all of the things that were kryptonite to a young, impressionable woman trying to find her way in the world.

In just a few days, he would show women "his way", whether it was on the sofa while the parents were away, downstairs in his father's mancave, in his Cherry Red Ford Mustang parked outside, or at one of the sleazy motels at the border of the city so they could be as loud as they wanted.

It was one of his ways of testing his body to see if the workouts he practiced at the gym worked. Douglas would spend the better part of the week at the gym, swearing to himself that he would never be pot-bellied like his father or like his younger brother, fat and somewhat disgusting as a human being. The 20-year old hottie tapped out just underneath him for a second.

"Time out, Dougie. Time out."

The slick sheen glinting off her body only made Douglas' dick harder. He hesitated on pulling out and slowed his pace.

"Time out, Doug!" Maggie pulled herself away, feeling his thickness slide out from in between her legs, her calves and thigh muscles quivering from being on high alert for such an extended amount of time.

"Need some water?"

Maggie turned to see Doug's statuesque form sitting on the sofa behind her, muscles glistening over from the sweat, his rigid member pulsing between his legs, still wanting to get at her for a little longer, his Adam Levine haircut still getting the best of her desire.

I need a five-minute break, at least. Reminder: Never go out with a guy who spends all day at the gym unless you're prepared for the consequences.

Maggie could already feel the soreness sinking into her body, the dull ache taxing her rather quickly. She felt as though she had worked out for those 30 minutes of simply fucking Doug.

Douglas made no attempt to get up and get her the water. Instead, he pointed in the direction of the kitchen and let his body relax on the couch.

"There's some bottled water in the fridge, second shelf down on the left. Get me a bottle, too, will ya?"

What an asshole!

But deep down inside, Maggie already knew that was going to be the case.

These spoiled, little rich boy types are always the same. It just comes with the turf, she reminded herself. After getting her bearings, Maggie did her best saunter in front of Douglas, keeping her ass tight and desirable.

Douglas didn't seem to notice. He was laid back against the back of the couch, his chin up, his eyes closed, the ceiling fan cooling him off from the little workout that they just had.

It figures, Maggie thought to herself, not bothering to continue to tighten those nearly perfect cheeks, making her way into the kitchen without a thought. Of course, she didn't expect to run into anyone in there at all, let alone a young nerd who didn't seem to know what to do when he saw a gorgeous, naked woman.

Tobias just stared in awe at the woman that manifested before him, the 2-liter of Mountain Dew still in his hand, his empty cup sitting on the counter not far from him, waiting to be filled. But then there was Maggie. She was a little surprised by him being there but couldn't stop what had already happened. She sauntered over to the fridge and opened it up, grabbing two bottles of water, simply glancing over at Tobias as she made her way back into the living room, Tobias staring hard at the Betty Boop tattoo she had on the outside of her thigh.

"Could you close the fridge for me?"

Tobias nodded and complied, blindly pushing the door shut with his free hand. It closed and he was left in the darkness again, listening to the sounds of two people who really wanted to fuck.

Too bad my life sucks, Tobias thought to himself. *Now on to tits and ass of another kind!*

Downstairs, in the man cave of all man caves, Mark and his crew laid in wait for the flashing title and intro song to come on for their favorite show, *Super Space Bounty Hunt: The Series*.

Already in its second season, a great nerd following had already become sucked into the storyline and its cast of characters; a lone space bounty hunter, wise in her ways, spends 45 minutes prancing around in a skin-tight leather outfit, complete with holsters and a set of mysterious space blasters that she got from her long-dead father, blah, blah, blah.

Tobias and the rest of them knew what they were watching; nerd porn. Like all the other sci-fi and fantasy television shows the last few generations, they pandered to the sexless intellectual, easily trapping Tobias and the others within the confines of this infrastructure at a fairly young age.

But *Super Space Bounty Hunt: The Series* teased on a whole different level than all of the other shows.

Last week, Captain Banda Pang and her space crew were jettisoned out of their trusty spacecraft, *The Enforcer*, Captain Pang crash landing in a pile of space slime, on a solo mission to get back to her crew. Soon, her skin-tight outfit was covered in sticky space slime, her curves and light blue skin covered in a stickiness of unknown origins, eating away at her space suit. She was forced to take all of her outfit off and clear her dirty, alien body.

The rest of her space crew were worlds away, the castaway enchantress finally able to bare her assets properly for the audience, unzipping the front of her flight suit to escape the confines of the slime before it devoured her as well. Just as her perk, alien breasts were about to pop out of the suit-commercial break.

Besides hearing Mark swear at the t.v. in a string of colorful profanity that was impressive even for him, Tobias and the others had to watch as the captain was suddenly clean of all slime and drying her hair after commercial break, continuing to break their spirit further.

However, this week promised to be the moment that they got to see-

"Titties! We're gonna see some titties!" Mark threw a mock celebration by letting a few Cheetos puffs go flying into the air around them, a few of them hitting his compatriots to the cause.

Mark stuffed a few of them in his mouth. "Sci-geek.com review for this episode says we'll finally get to see those perk beauties."

But Clark wasn't buying it. His matter of fact tone sobered all of Mark's excitement as well as some of the others that had gotten excited in the prospect of alien breasts.

"No, we're not, Mark. No matter how much we want to see the great rack the captain apparently has hidden beneath her myriad of fashionable spacewear, we'll never see them! The actress isn't paid enough and this is on a sci-fi station, which doesn't allow adult features to air on-" But Mark never got to respond. Rudely and without warning, the sanctity of their nerd domicile was interrupted.

"What's up, dorks?" It was Douglas. He was finished upstairs and his sweaty form bounded down the carpeted steps to the man cave, his eyes looking from one nerd to another.

Oh, no. Of all the places that he didn't want to be, Tobias knew that here during any movie marathon or t.v. show, he and the other nerd clan were in contact with the possibility of ridicule, noogies, wedgies, and an assortment of other asinine and juvenile tendencies when Douglas was here, but they suffered through it time and again nonetheless.

Mainly because Mark's dad had a great flat screen and sound system that would make even Gene Roddenberry nod in respect to the homage that was paid to quality sound and picture.

It was really like being in the movies, Tobias reminded himself, leaning back against the movie theater chair, trying his best to keep well hidden from Douglas. But, somehow, Douglas always found him. And he always seemed to be looking for him the most.

Maybe it was the way my underwear ripped or the squeak that came out of my throat when I felt my balls get pressed up against my pelvis during the wedgie, Tobias remarked dryly to himself, looking for a way out but finding only Mark's sweaty Calvin Klein model look-alike for a brother leering at him, mingled sex sweat nearly dried on him after the go around with the girl upstairs.

"So, you get a good look and file that one away, Tobe-ster?"

"Hey, Doug. What? File what away?"

"The creeper shot you got of my girl upstairs in the kitchen. I know you saw something you shouldn't have seen, dork!"

Fuck me! Now he has a reason to dig into me, Tobias squirmed uneasily a bit, trying his best to think of a fancy retort in which to be free from Douglas' captivity, but Tobias had nothing. Well, except this.

"I was just getting something to drink. I put my Mountain Dew in the fridge to keep it-"

Douglas mocked Tobias in his best nerd voice, pulling up his baggy jeans over his belly button.

"'I was just getting something to drink. I put my Mountain Dew-" Douglas snatched the 2-liter of Mountain Dew from Tobias' hands, turning it up next his lips. In a few deep gulps, half of the 2-liter was gone.

No one said anything. Their t.v. show played in the background, the obligatory tit shot missed by all because Mark's douche of a brother was acting, well, like a douche. Douglas tipped the 2-liter back down and handed it to Tobias, a bit of it sloshing out sloppily in the nerd's lap. Douglas leaned down to face the nerd- and let out the loudest burp Tobias had ever witnessed- right in his face.

"Buuuuuuurrrrrrpppp! How you like that one, Tobes?"

Tobias wiped a bit of spittle from his face that had got on him from the epic burp and began to close the top on his drink, saving the rest for later. That's when Douglas surprised him and licked the right side of his face.

"Here's a bit of what you're missing, dork. I just finished going down on her and man, was it messy down there when I was through!"

Tobias didn't know whether or not he wanted to throw up or light the licked side of his face on fire to cleanse it from its filth. Douglas moved away from him and tipped Clark's bowl of popcorn into the nerd's lap and went back upstairs.

"Enjoy your show, dim-wits!"

In another few seconds, the credits were rolling and their show was over. Mark cried out in exasperation.

"I missed her titties! Oh, hell no!"

And that's how Tobias' night ended; with cursing, the smell of another's sex on him, and the lack of seeing a great pair of breasts. Of course, he would know they were great because of the blogs posts on the Internet the next day.

Episode Two:

The Great Debate

In all of the worlds, in all of the moments of his life, Tobias knew no greater in his short, 18-year-old existence. It was the night before the Marvel Movie Marathon and Fan-Dome Comics and Collectibles was abuzz with talk of the movie to champ all movies; The Avengers.

After this, the world will not be the same, Tobias continued to tell himself, looking at all the extra Avengers merchandise stocked up on the endcaps, the new comic wall, and even a special standee with a collection of Marvel Milestones and other graphic novel collections stocked and overstocked. There were even a few standee characters of all The Avengers placed in strategic spots throughout the shop that had a price tag on them if anyone wanted a life-size Scarlett Johansson in black, patent leather. Yeah, that one was gone as soon as it was put out.

There was even stock in the back of the store just in case endcaps sold out. Tobias knew this because he had been volunteering since he was 16 at the comic store for trade and a little cash on the side, some of which he had saved up to buy his Marvel Marathon ticket weeks earlier. In fact, all of his friends had bought a ticket at the same time, all planning on going in costume to the 6-movie nerd fest that would be the start of their summer together.

What a way to begin the summer, Tobias thought to himself, *first high school graduation, now this.* He grabbed the empty boxes he had just emptied from the stock he put out of Marvel action figures. The entire section was stocked up now, filling up the rest of the action figure wall near front of the store. Not far from him, he could hear Mark doing his best to convince the rest of the group that Hulk was indeed the strongest of all superheroes and that they would see it showcased during The Avengers film tomorrow night.

"Hulk would tear Superman a new asshole, dork! There's no way that Supes could tangle with Hulk for even a few minutes without winding up a Kryptonian pretzel!"

Mark was pretty adamant on this topic. From the very beginning of Tobias and Marks' conversations six years ago when they met, Mark had never faltered on his undying love for the green-skinned outcast, something that all who frequented the comic book store attempted to test at some point in time.

A little bit more about Fan-Dome, though. The comic store had been an older comic store that had gone out of business, like all good businesses do that aren't appreciated by the populace of the surrounding area. Tobias hadn't been in the area then but he saw the old photos of what the store looked like before it had been converted by Thomas Winterman, Mark's dad. The old place looked more or less like a shithole, let's just say that. It was that eclectic mix of a comic store trying to be a record store that was rapidly going out of style with the technology age in full swing; it still had VHS tapes for fucks sake!

Mr. Winterman did well renovating the store. The layout was like this; the building was in the shape of an F if you could look at it from above the store itself. The entrance was housed at the bottom of the F; that's where the counter was housed on the right and the new figure shelves on the left. Immediately to the left after that were sets of shelves that sat just to the left of the center of the store, four great shelves that housed all of the graphic novels and other hard cover selections that weren't on a wall.

In regards to the wall; the new comic wall was to the left of those shelves, starting immediately after the last great shelf and stretching all the way to the end of the store. Marvel was first, independents next, then DC at the end. Both Marvel and DC had the biggest sections but the independent titles were varied and seemed to need their own space because there were so many.

Just across from the new release wall was he gaming section. It had it's own section separate from all the others, in the bottom vertical line of the F, with 8 long tables set up in rows for Magic: The Gathering, Heroclix, War Hammer and other games that only nerds had the ability to play, for the rules were varied and, many times, changed with the latest edition that came out.

Just past that was on the right was the vintage figure section.   Anything from The Tick carded figures to Sideshow collectible statues were housed here, the rest of the shelves sporting a plethora of figures from the 1980's all the way to the latest from the Previews catalog. Mr. Winterman tried to get a little bit of everything in his store. If it didn't sell in a quarter, he'd throw it on eBay and have something in its place as soon as possible. Some things he kept on the shelf while others he pushed out the door as quick as possible.

There were two round tables at the end of the new release wall that was a hang out area for those that wanted to read comics or discuss comic-based things. Also, there was a grand poster section at the corner of the store near the tables, with over 150 different posters for sale. Just to the right of the tables was the door to the office and the back stock area.

The store did great business. Mr. Winterman saw to that. There was a small community college that he would advertise for, having get-togethers and giveaways, always being able to hook a comic reader or two every time. He also cut deals with different businesses around the area, getting catered events and screening passes for his real collectors to most of the super-hero based events.

He would handle the budgeting and ordering of product while his oldest son Douglas would manage the advertising and layout of the store, his youngest son Mark working the register ever since he was out of high school three years ago. Tobias loved it here. It was his home away from home, his sanctuary, his second family, as well as his-

Just then, the electric bell of the door rang and in walked another customer; the Goth chick. It wasn't a stereotype at all; it was more of typecasting because no one in Tobias' group knew the young woman's name.

She had gone to their high school and graduated a year earlier than Tobias' senior class. But, for the sake of argument, no one knew her name. Even Mark called her Goth chick whenever she wasn't around as they were referring to some of the regular hotties that came into the store.

And Goth chick was a regular, Tobias knew that for a fact. She had been coming to the comic store every Wednesday for the last few years and she was a mad fan of most of the gritty, independent titles; and, of course, anything that had Neil Gaiman's name on it.

She strolled into the store without making eye contact with the crew and Mark didn't bother to greet her as he was supposed to everyone that came in, per the rules of his father's store. Mark was an ass like that.

Even when he had a chance to talk to a girl, he fucked it up by being himself, the asshole of legend.
44

Mark continued, wrapping up his victory in a nice, little bow for all to see.

"If anything, Amalgam comics and the crossover fights that they did back in 96 was weak as shit! Those were PG-13 fights based upon submission. The best matches were determined by the fans! By the fans, Tobe-meister! Give me a fucking break!" Mark looked around at the others, somewhat befuddled.

"Anyone remember a character named Jason Todd and how his ending turned out when put in the hands of fans?" The group got quiet again. Mark always won these matches when it came to his prize favorite character, Hulk.

Goth chick arrived at the counter with her purchases. She didn't get a chance to say anything though, before Mark started in, asking for further victory from strangers.

"Who do you think would win, Goth chick, Superman or Hulk?"

She looked up at him, completely disinterested.

"Superman, I'm pretty sure, but I don't really read those titles."

"Superman, are you kidding me? He could get flicked by Hulk and-"

"I'm sorry, but I really don't care. Box # 98, please."

"Hey, just humor me here for a minute." Mark didn't know when to quit. He could see that she didn't really want to listen to his rants like the others around him but he pushed the issue.

"How about I don't and you get my box instead? Box # 98, please!"

Mark looked around at his friends for some back up. He found none. They were just surprised that Goth chick had said something, let alone to Mark. Usually, she just says her box number and then leaves with her merch.

"Hey, what's up with the attitude? I'm just trying to get an opinion here. You said Superman would win; I just want to know why you think that."

Then the conversation went from zero to sixty in 3.5 seconds. Tobias and the others could see that the young woman was perturbed. They just didn't expect her to strike so quick.

"You're a Comic Nazi!" No one saw that one coming. With that said, the whole group at the comic store got quiet. Even the pages of the comic books that were in mid-turn by random customers around them seemed to slow down.

What an accusation! But I'm sure she'll have back up.

For months, the Goth chick had come into the comic store and bought her merch and left, never bothering anyone. And every week she came in, Mark tried to get at her, tried to flirt with the inner slut that he thinks every woman has inside her.

Well, he called forth the thunder. And the thunder answered.

"Every day I come in here to pick up my comics and every day you pull some macho-ass line out of your ass at the checkout, thinking it will impress me enough to drop my panties for you. Well, it doesn't! And you have to have more than just something in your pants to get with me…. Or anyone else for that matter."

"Hey, Goth chick, what's your problem?" But Mark, not knowing that every line that he spouted out of his mouth made him sound more and more of an asshole, didn't use problematic inflection when delivering it to her.

And the fact that he called her Goth chick and not the name that was on her hold box probably didn't help too much either, Tobias thought to himself, closing the Green Lantern graphic novel to get a better viewing of the ass chewing that was about to take place.

"You behind the counter is my problem, fucker!"

Nice use of the word 'fucker'.

"You're a Comic Nazi because of the disdain that you have for every comic that is not oozing with tits and ass and full of 'roided up, testosterone-filled would-be heroes. Everything that is not in your cookie cutter ideal is spat upon, even when you know, in your heart of hearts, it's a good comic!"

"Listen Goth chick-"

"It's Cassidy, you underpaid miscreant!"

"Um, Cassidy- Wait, how do you know I'm underpaid?"

"Because you take it out on the populace around you that you're unhappy in your life situation." Cassidy, the Goth chick, waved her hand around at the rest of us, motioning to the entire comic book store as well, the rest of us still in awe that she said more than her famous two words she was used to saying.

This was an epic fuck you, if anything, Tobias thought, propping himself up on the cash register on the counter, listening intently at the verbal bashing. Of course, Tobias kept an air of unabashed insultedness plastered on his face as to not look like he was fully enjoying every moment of this.

"Box # 98. Look, Mark, I know you're a pathetic human being and you are unhappy about the choices or lack of choices that you've made along the way in the road that you so pathetically call your life, but there's no reason to dampen the spirits of others in a happy place like a comic book shop."

Cassidy sat the other purchases that she had acquired from the rest of the comic store and waited for her box.

50

And the only thing that Mark had to say, the only thing that he could say, which was an awful comeback, was:

"Fuck you, Goth chick! I knew you were a bitch!"

This and the many other things that Mark had said to her over the months of her shopping here had slid right off of her tough exterior, a slight half-smile showing at the corners of her mouth.

"And I don't want you in here anymore, Goth chick. Consider your box emptied and cancelled!"

She answered back calmly, taking her change and her comics.

"You can't really do that, now can you? You're not in a management position and I haven't said anything but the truth." Cassidy looked over to the rest of us that stood there, still stupefied that she had dealt Mark such a deadening blow. "Isn't that right, boys?"

We didn't say anything, though crowd-deafening applause or bowing down to her greatness would have been sufficient enough. We just stood there, our

little nerd hard-ons hidden well inside of our pants.

Episode Three:

Last night of Normal

"Dude, you could have at least backed me up, Tobes!" Mark dropped the register till and receipts into the deposit bag and closed the cash register back. It was closing time and everyone had gone, Mark still licking his wounds from the defeat in front of the crew at the hands of Goth chick, a.k.a. Cassidy. It was quite a defeat. She was the one walking out the door with a smile on her face. Of course, all of the crew were smiling on the inside, happy for a change that Mark was finally silenced for once.

And by a female, no less. Tobias tried to keep a straight face when responding. So far, he had to look away when talking about Cassidy. After it started raining, the rest of the crew left and only Mark and Tobias were left in the store until it closed.

"What did you want me to say, Mark? She would have chewed me a new asshole, too! And I don't have the chops for retaliation like you do!" Mark nodded in agreement.

"Damn straight you don't!" Mark laughed out loud.

This was the ritual. Every Tuesday and Wednesday night, Tobias would stay and assist Mark with the prep and clean up of the store until Mark finished counting the till and filing it away for the deposit in the safe in the office. It had been like that for over a year, Mr. Winterman completely comfortable with Tobias staying after close.

Mark put on the Empire Records soundtrack on the overhead speaker system, jamming *A Girl Like you*, by Edwyn Collins. He walked to the back of the store and into the office, which he had propped open by a long box of comics so he could hear the music while he was in there.

"Hey, Tobias! Can you get these boxes and take them to the recycling bin outside while I'm counting the till?"

Tobias looked out the window at the parking lot. It was pouring down outside. And Tobias knew that he would have to get something to cover him or he would get wet as well.

Definitely poncho weather, he concluded.

The comic store kept a coat and umbrella rack inside the office and Mark kept an old, raggedy camouflage poncho hanging there just in case. Tobias made his way back to the office after he finished stocking the sodas in the cooler.

"You so totally owe me, you know that, right? It's raining like crazy out there."

Mark was busy counting the money and credit card slips and didn't bother to answer. Tobias shrugged it off and slipped into the poncho, putting the hood up over his head to cover him as completely as possible. He grabbed the first round of boxes, opened the office door exit wide, and threw them out into alleyway. He did the same with the rest of the boxes until there weren't anymore, letting himself out. The door shut and clicked behind him.

Outside, the rain blew in from the side, soaking Tobias' jeans and shoes in just a few seconds of being outside.

Whatever happened to April showers bringing May flowers? Apparently that rhyme doesn't mean jack! The young man grabbed the first set of boxes and began walking them down the alleyway. In another few seconds, he saw the recycle dumpster next to the singled out garbage cans. He tossed the boxes into the open door. They fell in with a boom, echoing loudly inside the dumpster. He went back for the rest.

56

"Super owe me, Mark!" But Mark couldn't hear him. The door was closed, he was counting money, and the music was on. He grabbed a second load of boxes, sloshing his way back to the dumpster. The rain was coming in from the side, the wind picking up around him, spraying his face with a thick mist.

That's when he heard something. It sounded like something had moved within the drainage pipes connected to the wall next to him. Tobias moved away from the wall, toting the boxes, when he felt something hit him in the head.

"Ouch! Son of a bitch!" He sidestepped away and looked up into the sky to see where it came from. All he could see was the streetlight and a cascading curtain of water that nearly blinded him when he lifted his covered head up to see. He heard a splash behind him.

He turned around quickly, nearly dropping the boxes.

"Alright, Mark! Enough playing around! You know I don't like pranks like this." Many times, Mark had set up an elaborate prank to scare people in his crew.

But Tobias heard nothing else, except for the rain, which kept its steady beat on him and the rest of the world. Tobias waited another moment for a second sound, rubbing the top of his head where that something had hit him. He continued what he was doing, dropping the rest of the boxes into the bin. On his way back, that's when Tobias realized what had struck him.

It was a box. A small, black, rectangular box, *no bigger than a cigar box*, Tobias noticed. It was sitting in a puddle not far from where he had been struck. He looked up into the sky, trying to see over the top of the comic shop, to see if it had come from another prankster, but he could see nothing.

He picked up the box. It was made out of wood and it was rather light, Tobias noticed, wiping the
58

rain off of it. It had no markings, no symbol or lock or slit to place your fingers on and open it.

"I wonder what's in it." Tobias tried to get it open but couldn't seem to manage it. He slipped it under the poncho and kept it hidden as he walked back into the office door.

Mark was finishing at the desk, putting the receipts and cash into a deposit bag, making the last of his markings on the nightly deposit logs. He was still jamming, but to *Crazy Life* by Toad the Wet Sprocket.

"Well, I'm done, Mark. All the boxes are tossed."

Mark turned down the music from his seat on the controls in front of him.

"You ready, my friend?"

"Ready? Ready for what?"

"Marvel Movie Marathon, mother fucker! Five, count 'em, five movies that culminate into a final, great collaboration of superheroes entitled-" he paused, "The Avengers!"

"Yeah, sure, man." Mark turned back around in the swivel chair, closing the logbooks and tossing the deposit bag into the safe by his feet. Tobias took this moment to pull off the still-dripping poncho and slide the unknown box into his comic bag next to his light windbreaker on the table near him. He hung up the poncho on a coat hook and picked up his things.

"You're still going as Iron Man, right Tobias? Cause I found this killer Hulk costume and Clark and Junior already have their Cap and Thor gear ready to go. Remember, we're going to meet there at 10:30 a.m. There's supposed to be all this cool merch available and I don't want it to run out."

"I'm there, man. Clark's supposed to be picking me up. Mom has to use the car tomorrow."

"Fucking A! I'll see you then."

"Yep. Until then." Mark finished straightening up and Tobias grabbed his things, making his way for the front door. His heart was beating fast for some reason. Maybe it was the fact that he decided to keep the box a secret just to himself until he found out what it was or maybe it was the fact that his mind was reeling at the possibilities at what it could be.

All the way home in his mother's car, he looked over at the black box. He had taken it out of the comic bag so it wouldn't get his comics wet and so he could look at it. It was just a short drive to the apartment complex they lived in, but the minutes seemed to drag. Soon, Tobias pulled into the parking lot and put the car in park, shut it off and grabbed his things. He tucked everything under the windbreaker he wore and rushed to the door.

His mother wasn't home yet. It was only 10:15 from what the wall clock in the dining room said. *She wouldn't be home for another hour or so,* Tobias managed, slipping off his wet shoes and darting into his bedroom.

He dropped all his things on the bed, slipped out of his windbreaker, tossing it on the floor, and sat the box down on his computer table, clearing away some of the debris so he could see.

What was in it? Who gave it to me? How do you open it?

Once he sat down, Tobias noticed that the box wasn't black at all. It was dark, yes, but a dark brown at best.   And it seemed to stave off the water completely, still remaining dry though it had been sitting in a puddle. And he noticed something else, too. There **was** a button. He had missed it looking at it in the rain. It wasn't a button exactly, but it was a button of sorts. In between the seams of the wood, there was a small sliver of metal that poked out, barely a hair's breadth further than rest of the box itself. Tobias pressed it in with his finger- and the box popped open. The young man leaned back, half expecting a miniature Gremlin to pop out or for there to be some booby trap on it. But there was none. There was simply a glow that broke from the edges of the box; a light blue glow. The more Tobias opened the box, the stronger the glow became, until he could see inside what made the glow.

It was a bag of pills. Small in size and completely see-through, a large quantity of them sat in a clear plastic bag, tucked tightly in the box. He opened the box the rest of the way up so that the lid propped itself open and lifted the bag out of the box carefully.

Underneath the bag, there was a small, square card the size of a business card. Nothing was printed on the front of it but, as Tobias flipped it over, he noticed there was writing on the other side. It read the following:

To the procurer of these pills, use wisely and with moderation.

And that was it. That's all it read. He looked for other things inside, for a secret compartment in the small, rectangular box, but found nothing. *Just a bag of glowing pills and a warning note.*

He took out one of the pills and sat it in the palm of his hand. He squeezed it a bit with his fingers.

It didn't feel like any pill that I've ever seen before. The exterior to the pill wasn't a gel cap at all like he thought. *It looked more like a silicone base.*

He sat it in the light in front of him, looking at it, then at the bag full of them, then at the note.

Did some drug dealer drop their stash? No, that can't be it because it fell from the roof and it had a note in it. It was even stored in a classy, black box. So, it's not some science experiment. It would be at a medical lab at not at the local comic shop.

Tobias was no fool. He didn't just take random drugs like so many of his generation. Sure, he had dabbled in weed from time to time with some of his friends, but never anything stronger for fear that it would mess up his brain and the rest of this body.

What's the worst that one could do?

He popped one into his mouth and dry swallowed it.

After ten minutes, Tobias didn't feel any different so he went to bed.

So much for the pill, Tobias thought to himself.

But the young man had no idea what was in store for him.

Episode Four:

With great self-esteem...

May 3rd, 2012... every comic book nerd's dream. The fact of the matter is that we were actually there.

"Oh my fucking shit, I'm about to come in my pants again! Free merch!" Mark's couth was always unsettling, but it never was so bad as it had been at the Marvel Movie Marathon that night as they stood in line at the entrance of the movieplex to see The Avengers for the first time.

The screening of five, count'em, five Marvel movies that led up to the pinnacle; The Avengers at 12:01! For any comic book fan or fan of superhero movies, this was a day that they had been preparing for. They couldn't simply just go see The Avengers at 12:01. It was a team thing that had them paying 40 dollars for all six movies.

Iron Man, The Incredible Hulk, Iron Man 2, Thor, and Captain America: The First Avenger were all screened first, the marathoners using a lanyard-based system to get them in and out of the theater on frequent bathroom breaks, refills on drinks and popcorn, as well as the breaks that were placed between each movie so the projectionist could set up the next movie.

Mark already had his Hulk 3-D glasses on, sitting atop his head, a small handful of the same free comic sitting next to the set of double-sided mini posters of each character. He was set; happy would be a better word.

In a very brief span of moments, Tobias had seen Mark happy. It came down to these three things; trade/convention events, new comic release days, and knowing he was going to get laid. The fact that Mark had been stuck at the comic book shop every time the owner took to a convention with his back stock of comics as well as other things he did not sell over the quarter, Mark was hanging on comic release days to make him happy; because there was no way that he was getting sex from any woman.

You could see it in his stare, in the way that Mark still had that child-like view in his eyes; something that Tobias felt he had let go of some time ago. But Tobias didn't have sex either. He dreaded thinking about the one time that he did have sex and wished it away several times, only wanting to look ahead and not back at that awful experience.

Most of his friends had understood the experience quite well and sympathized with him but it left his libido scarred for some time after that.

They understand, sure, Tobias thought, *but do they really care?* Tobias decided some time ago that the rest of his friends were dealing with the same thing, if not more than what he was dealing with in regards to socialization and "meeting of the proverbial girl that would consider fucking you". Tobias looked around at the crowd that gathered inside the midnight screening of The Avengers and knew that he had a problem immediately.

All around him, there were freaks of nature. Men that looked like 300 pound children dressed in jeans and a comic book superhero t-shirt, complete with disheveled hair and acne that should have gone away during the mid-20's but didn't.

There were women that were somewhat androgynous, forming a hodge-podge sort creation that looked male but had long hair and some feminine features. The only thing that kept them apart from the overweight males was the fact that the women wore bras to house their titties and the men didn't.

Then there were the Peter Pan girls; the girls that never really matured into women. Somehow, lost amidst the comic-book generation, women in their late teens and early twenties were regular Jane Van Dyne's, sporting a short hair cropped around the face and a chest and ass almost as flat as their first day of high school.

It wasn't that they were ugly, Tobias could agree to that easily enough. Many of them were Ellen Page gorgeous. He had masturbatory fantasies about women like this all the time. Just the other day, he had masturbated to the idea of one of the comic book girls that came to the store on the regular. It was some rather quick, broad strokes, but it got the job done nonetheless.

But what it was, for Tobias anyway, was the fact that there were those that were lost in a world of things that made sense easily enough around them. All of the freaks of nature that he knew were smart, funny, witty, and charismatic, making for a good friend or at least familiar acquaintance.

Tobias even found himself wondering what these people were going to do once they had to grow up fully and experience life for what it really was; a sad, pathetic little trail of memories and experiences that culminate with you losing bowel control constantly until you just don't give a fuck about anything anymore. Tobias just couldn't see some 80-year-old man in a senior citizen home wearing a Spiderman shirt and cargo shorts.

Indeed, Tobias thought, *things will have to change for them soon.*

Thor's nudge and smile brought Tobias back from his momentary daze.

"Check her out, Iron Man. Oh my god, are those ta-tas fantastic!"

Tobias' gaze grazed over the 6 o'clock destination that Thor had spied with his delightfully pervy but very accurate eye. An equally nerdy girl, though quite hot, was dressed up in Black Widow cosplay, sporting a skin-tight suit from which her chest was nearly bursting out of, the small zipper placed strategically in between her breasts doing its best to hold the suit together.

They were fantastic, without a doubt. The girl's skin was a pale white, a few red freckles dotting the tops of her cleavage, the freckles matching her red hair that was trimmed just like Scarlett Johansen's in the Avengers film they were about to see.

"She's paid to be here, Thor."

Thor seemed taken aback.

"Why do you say that? She could just as easily be here like the rest of us, going to see The Avengers like half the world is doing right now."

"No, I've seen her before. Remember last year's Free Comic Book Day?"

"Yes, I was first in line."

"Remember the girl that Fan-Dome got to model outside holding a sign for free comics? The one dressed as Power Girl?"

Thor nodded.

"That's her- but without the blond wig."

Thor stared a few moments longer, his eyes redefining the dimensions of the woman in front of them getting a refill on her soft drink. Soon, Thor's eyes grew wide.

"You're good, Iron Man!"

"That's why I'm Iron Man." A sudden urgency declared a state of emergency in Tobias' bladder.

"Hey, can you tell Hulk and Captain America that I'll be back. I'm just going to the bathroom." Clark smiled under the blond Thor wig and waved a foam Mjolnir high over his head.

"It shall be done, Iron Man! By Odin's beard, it shall be done!"

This is why I'm never going to get laid. I hang around Clark far too much. And he's still a virgin.

Tobias was nearly smothering in the Iron Man costume, the fake muscles probably made of some kind of cotton, insulating him more than just a regular costume. He needed to take a breather for a moment, and then he'd be back for The Avengers, raring and ready to go.

The young man dodged through the crowd of moviegoers for a brief stint at the bathroom then to get a box of Milk Duds at the concession stand before returning. He took a quick pee break and took off the Iron Man costume. The only thing that he could do was slide out of the top. It was made like a mechanics one piece, with a few dabs of Velcro to hold it together in the back. Underneath, Tobias wore a pair of loose-fitting boxers and an Avengers shirt. He went to wash his hands and noticed that he was soaked through with sweat, his Avengers shirt damp with sweat.

"Remind me to never wear a costume like this for eight hours straight!" He fanned the shirt with some paper towels, even trying to soak up some of the sweat. In the end, he let the upper portion hang down so his shirt could air out, walking back out to the main lobby and on his way to the concession stand. He was in line for only a minute or so when he felt a hand tap him on the shoulder.

"I'm Maggie. Remember me?"

Scantily clad in a short, black skirt and a dark black Batman t-shirt that barely fit her ample curves, it would be hard for Tobias to forget something as amazing as a picture as this. But he didn't remember her, not at all.

"No, I can't say that I remember you...Maggie."

The moment a hot girl talks to you and you're dressed up as a super hero, the dumber you feel wearing it. That's just a rule of super hero costumes.

You don't try to hit on a girl while in a super hero costume. You can hit on them while they're wearing one because it's like they're wearing a sex suit, but you can't hit on them while you're wearing one.

Tobias didn't make the rules, he just knew that those had always been the unwritten rules of costumes.

"I was with Douglas the other day, at his house."

Douglas. Oye, another one of his women, Tobias thought. But then Maggie flashed a little bit of thigh and the Betty Boop tattoo was there, just like it had been when she had come sauntering into the kitchen and left Tobias with a massive erection that he had to take care of later that night. It was clear now where he knew her; she was being plowed by Doug's dick that day.

"Oh, yes. I'm sorry. I didn't recognize you with clothes on."

Did that just come out of my mouth?

"Yep, that was me." Maggie moved in closer, her skirt now back down around her tanned thighs, the Batman shirt, though not Marvel, was at least an effort on her part to be a part of something greater than herself; it wasn't working too well. She was just a hottie in a sea of virgins. Tobias continued with the conversation, noting that the other nerds in line for popcorn and soda were looking at him with that, 'Is that your sister' look that all unbelieving nerds have when other nerds talk to pretty women. The line moved forward a bit more, Tobias trying to continue conversation with her but very aware at how close it was until The Avengers started.

"Wow, so you're a superhero fan, huh?"

"Why would you say that?"

"Well, you've got a super hero t-shirt on and you're here to see The Avengers at the midnight showing."

"Oh, I'm just here with Doug."

Suddenly, Tobias' eyes went to scanning the sector around him, waiting for a surprise visit from Mark's older brother, complete with a headlock and noogies or a wedgie that ripped Tobias' underwear in half. But there was no Doug to be found. Maggie seemed to notice Tobias looking around.

"Oh, Doug went back to the comic store to get the passes for tonight. He left them."

"Oh, that's too bad. You might miss the first couple of minutes of the movie. And the trailers are supposed to be epic, too."

"Would you mind missing them with me?"

There was something in her eyes, something that brought a jolt to the young man's system. It was hard to describe and Tobias didn't try. He was still stuck on what she had said.

'Would you mind missing them with me?' And she said that to ME.

Those-seven-glorious-words. Stan Lee could form no better words on a comic book page if he tried. The beauty was there, the offer was there. Whatever the offer was, Tobias knew that he would take it, no matter how bad the beating he got from Doug afterwards. There were months that would pass that Tobias would dream of a situation like this, usually a fantasy filled with random women that he would find attractive along the way in his journey through the mall, through his high school, or even standing in line at the supermarket with his mother. The thoughts would always start like this then they would push his teen mind further and further into depravity, something he needed very badly at the moment.

"I'm sorry, what did you say?"

"I want to show you something." Those-six-words. Stan Lee wouldn't dare write anything better on a comic book page, knowing that he would be booed off the stage of the world, not allowing a young nerd to find solace in the arms of a beautiful woman when it was most needed.

And there was something in her eyes, something that glossed over her eyes a bit, making them look like fine marbles, her smile penetrating Tobias' insides, making them somewhat mushy quite easily.

"I-I don't know. Where- where would we go?"

Tobias had never envisioned a bathroom stall as a location in which good sex could occur, always noting that the scenes in movies that this happened; it was always in slow motion.

The world was not in slow motion, the young man told himself, watching as Maggie peeled off her panties from under the skirt, dropping them to the floor.

The world was moving too fast, Tobias thought, but he didn't have time to think about it much before Maggie's hands were on his costume, pulling it off in seconds, his white shirt and boxers underneath the only thing he was wearing.

"I want to fuck you so bad right now!"

It wasn't a dream, it was real. Very real. Maggie's breasts popped out of the Batman shirt with ease, no bra underneath, her delicious breasts in his face as she grabbed at his dick in his boxers. Tobias was rock hard, just from the conversation in the concession line. He was beyond rock hard when her hand found him, her fingers wrapping tightly around it as she moved herself down onto him.

"God, I'm so turned on right now! I don't know what it is, but I'm about to come and we haven't even fucked yet."

Tobias didn't say anything, nothing at all. He just enjoyed the moment. His breathing was just as ragged as hers as she slid her moistness down onto his rigid member, both of them moaning out as they braced themselves inside the stall, Tobias' feet firmly on the floor, one hand on the seat protector dispenser and the other on the toiler paper holder, Maggie with her arms wrapped around his neck, her tennis shoes braced just behind Tobias, on the back of the toilet.

Tobias could smell her perfume; thick and rich. *Probably expensive*, he thought, pressing himself deeper into her the wetter she became, watching her face contort in pleasure as she began a pace, something Tobias had trouble following without the urgency of his orgasm playing on his mind almost immediately.

"Stop-slow down, you're going to make me come!" That was the only thing that he could bring himself to say to her.

"Isn't that the point- oh my god- I'm coming! Ooooooohhh!"

Tobias could feel her release all over him, the front of his boxers taking most of the punishment. Maggie continued to move over him, her hips sinking down onto his lap. Tobias could feel the intensity build up inside of him, the tip of his dick about to explode with pleasure. He grabbed Maggie and pulled her closer, biting down on one of her nipples. She squealed out and tightened up on him, Tobias' surge rushing forward.

"I'm coming, Maggie! I'm-com-ing..."

His words fumbled, his mind exploded, among other things. Maggie squeezed her moistness around his shaft as he exploded deep inside of her, her panting mouth on his neck, tongue licking the small dabs of sweat that dribbled down back behind his left ear. The young man shook in delight and, when his vision cleared, he noticed a small gathering of feet outside the stall, standing in one place.

But Maggie was still there, half-naked and filled with what passion Tobias had for her, some of her dark hair plastered to her face while a few hairs stood up unevenly on her head, making her almost look like a real woman for a second.

He fumbled for words. They didn't find his lips at first, many of them still caught in his throat along the way to her.

"I..Maggie...thank—" Maggie's lips stopped him from speaking.

It was better this way, Tobias decided, taking her in his arms, his hands awkwardly groping for a hold around her to steady himself. He was still inside of her and his sensitivity meter was still going off.

Maggie pressed him down onto the toilet, his back accidentally flushing the toilet in response. Suddenly, the feet around the stall scattered and scooted away, but they did not leave, they simply made room for those in the stall to exit.

Maggie pressed her lips against Tobias', kissing him hard. She moved her lips to his ear and whispered to him.

"That was amazing. Just what I needed." She climbed off of him then, straightening her skirt down around her thighs and putting her shirt back over those near-perfect breasts. She opened the stall door before Tobias had a chance to recover, stepping outside.

"Excuse me. I think I walked into the wrong bathroom." Tobias could see her legs move past the others standing just outside. Tobias pulled his superhero suit back on and pulled the cloth Iron Man helmet out of his pocket, putting it on. He straightened up as best as he could and walked out to face the crowd.

An eruption of applause began once he exited, being caught off guard how many guys there actually were in the bathroom listening. He got pats on the back, high fives, and numerous accolades before he walked back out into the lobby.

By now, he knew that the movie had already started, but he was still out of breath and trying to get himself together. He bought the Milk Duds simply as an alibi and walked in just as Loki escaped in the back of a S.H.I.E.L.D. vehicle with Hawkeye and the others. Tobias ducked down and sat down next to Thor, taking off his Iron Man mask. He breathed a sign of relief.

Thor looked disapprovingly at him.

"You're late, Iron Man! Okay, here's what you missed. First-"

But Tobias' mind was on other things.

Naked, writhing things. Things named Maggie that made his summer only 1,000 times better than it ever could have been.

Episode Five:

The Morning After

"I was with a woman last night!" No matter how much Tobias convinced the mirror version of himself standing in front of him, he was having trouble believing it himself. He still felt the numbness, the tingle that his body has when it has sex. He had only felt it one other time.

It's as if there's an electrical charge between two people. And boy, was there a charge between me and whatever her name was!

And it was in that moment that Tobias realized he had cheap and meaningless sex. And he wasn't upset. In fact, he was proud of himself.

And so were the fifteen other guys outside the stall, he reminded himself, distinctly remembering the cheers he got when he came out of the stall afterwards...

Dammit, why can't I remember her name?

Tobias, not able to remember anything but the graphic depiction of what good sex was like on his lap, her tight Batman tee hugging her breasts together and the feeling she gave him rather quickly. Tobias decided to call her Betty in his mind, after the sexy tattoo she familiarized him with at the theater. Personally, he didn't think he would be talking about this with anyone in the near future. He could have said something to Clark but he chose not to and just relished in the moment.

After all, it was mine to have and enjoy, right? Tobias' mind then drifted to the most obvious question of all, the one that stuck out like a sore thumb.

Why me? Why in the world would she choose me out of the crowd? She knew me, sure, but only because I was in line at the concession stand and happened to see her in all her glory with Doug on the living room couch the other night.

Tobias made a mental note right then that he wouldn't be sitting on any of Mark's home furniture anytime in the near future.

Then he spied the box that had fallen on him the other night and remembered the pills inside.

The drugs did it! The pill somehow turned her on! But that was impossible!

In comic books, crazier things have been known to happen. In Spiderman's origins, he was bitten by a radioactive spider, the Joker had a chemical bath in toxic sludge. For Hal Jordan, it was the power ring given to him by an interplanetary police alien that patrolled the galaxy and was near death and in need of a replacement. The entire team of the Fantastic

Four had been changed by radiation from space and Bruce Banner's transformation was caused by overexposure to gamma radiation.

They all had some influence on their bodies that made it take upon a change of sorts, resulting in their superpower.

But what did the Pill do to me? And how did it affect Betty without me even touching her? Tobias had seen a classic 90's film called Love Potion # 9 in which the parties (played by Tate Donovan and a young Sandra Bullock) ingest a love potion and simply speak to the opposite sex and the fun ensues.

But she spoke to me first! And she propositioned ME!

So, what did I do? I know it wasn't the costume. The Iron Man muscle suit did nothing to make him look any hunkier or attractive to the ladies. If anything, it made him look like an oversized child. After all, Tobias couldn't find a costume that would fit his long legs, which made the costume look even worse on him.

And she didn't even know the difference between Marvel and DC, let alone that The Avengers was a Marvel film.

Tobias decided it was best to list the steps up to his meeting with Betty.

1. Left theater to go to the bathroom, loosened costume so it could air out
2. Got into concession line for more snacks
3. Ran into "Betty"
4. Was propositioned/accepted proposition
5. Was fucked senseless in the bathroom

Tobias smiled at #5 on the list. Five steps into Google, Tobias discovered how it had occurred. It was through his sweat. He was sweaty underneath the costume and, when he went to open it up to air it out, the pill's effects escaped through the pheromones created in his body. In reality, everyone gives off some type of chemical reaction through his or skin. Their smell either disgusts or tantalizes another individuals. *Perfume and cologne companies use this method all the time in order to sell their product, so why wouldn't this be possible?*

This was incredible! This pill, these pills, give me superpowers!

Tobias held up the box of pills above his head, letting the moment sink in, his own victory moment recorded in his head for future reference.

Now, the question was how many did he have left?

He poured the bag out on his computer desk and began the count.

2-4-6-8-10-12...

After a minute or so, he came up with the final tally.

Forty-nine pills left. I better make them count. Tobias had no idea who would give him such a power or that whether or not he could handle it. Simply just being eighteen with hormones raging during this time was trouble. Already, his mind was filling up with questions that couldn't be answered.

He would have to test out his theory further, take the pill and see how a person reacts. Study the symptoms, journal about the responses that are given to the taker of the pill. Tobias would have to have sex-with women-who wanted to!

The idea of being able to have sex and the other person completely willing and full of desire just as Betty had been made Tobias' mind swim with the possibilities.

But where would he start? Where is the perfect place for this kind of experiment to take place?

Then he heard his mother's voice from downstairs.

"Tobias, come on! If we're going to the gym, let's go."

Light bulb! Tobias would start at the gym. There were countless numbers of women there and they were all hot and sweaty. It was a common occurrence to be dripping with sweat. That way Tobias could test his theory about the pheromones.

Tobias pulled on his black workout shorts and his short running shirt, slipping on his running shoes from his early days at track last year. He could hear his mother getting ready for their morning workout routine that they did together ever since he found out he was going away to college three months ago. He was happy that he didn't have to get up early in the morning since he had graduated, so 10 a.m. wasn't impossible for him, especially since he wasn't working during the summer, with the exception of volunteering at Fan-Dome Comics and Collectibles.

He popped two of the pills in his mouth and met his mother downstairs, grabbing his water bottle before the two of them left. He took a few gulps of water from it and swallowed the two pills down.

Here we go. First experiment. Let's see if these are for real!

Fitness Paradise was a 24 hours gym, complete with a full locker room that had changing rooms, showers, lockers, and changing stalls. You used a keycard/key fob for entrance and Tobias had found himself here many nights by himself, running on the treadmills after high school was out, still having the running fever about no longer being in track.

The gym had weight machines and free weights in the back part of the gym and cardio machines such as bicycles, treadmills, and elliptical machines set up in the front of the windows so the runners could look out at the rest of the world as it went by.

Ever since his mother had recovered from breast cancer, she took it upon herself to get healthy and stay healthy. She had never been unhealthy before, but she made sure that the life she had left was accounted for and not wasted at all. His mother got her a gym membership and a monthly trainer there that would help keep her on track and help her set goals. As soon as they entered the gym, that's where his mother went off to.

"Remember, I'm training for the Run for Awareness campaign with my support group. The 5K is only a few days away."

"Gotcha, mom. You want me to pace with you on the treadmills today?"

But his mother shook her head.

"I don't think so today. I have my workout with my trainer. But in the next few days I need you to pace with me at least two times, once here and once on a track outside, okay?"

"Okay."

"Enjoy your workout." And then his mom disappeared into the gym.

"I will, mom. I will."

After stretching out, Tobias made a beeline for the treadmills. There were over 30 treadmills, with two rows of 15 in them. Many of them were already filled in the first row near the window, but he wasn't looking for convenience. He was looking for-

There she was. Everyday he went to the gym with his mother, he always spied this young woman, early twenties, running by herself. Many times, he would get a treadmill next to her just to keep pace and see how long it would take for her to slow down.

But she must have been a runner, too, Tobias decided, always noticing her strong calves and thighs plodding away at her daily run. She would be covered in sweat and most of her gym clothes would have sweat trails on them by the time she was finished on the treadmill.

However, she looked like she was just starting. Tobias found the treadmill to the left of her available and hopped on, beginning his warm up jog. He smiled over at her but she was in the zone, ear buds, arms swinging at her sides.

She was a blond, with short hair that was up in a little pony tail, a small trail of blond hairs trailing down her neck, some wisps of hair that didn't make it into the ponytail hanging down all on their own. She wore a pair of baby blue track shorts and a matching string gym top, a pair of track shoes, and an armband that held her smartphone. She was all business.

There was no way that I could get her attention, let alone ask her out on a date. She was too mature and too grown up for the likes of me, Tobias thought to himself. *I'm just a nerd that likes comics and lives with his mom.* And Tobias knew then that his life sounded like the beginning of bad fiction about a serial killer, a washed-up loser, or that guy that never took a chance in life. *Take your pick, I've got little going for me at this moment.*

100

Of course, in reality, Tobias' life was just starting. There was no need for him to get down on himself. Much had gone on that had slowed his track of life down; the absence of his father at an early age, his mother battling cancer, Tobias having to take on the father role in his own home at thirteen. All of these things did not hinder his growth in anyway. In fact, they simply enhanced his character.

Tobias kept a pretty even pace for the first five minutes, getting his warm up out of the way. Once the silent timer went off on the treadmill, his full workout began, a series of hills and slopes, Tobias' legs going to work as they had during his days at track. Without breaking his stride, he was able to hold for 10 minutes straight, his body beginning to sweat.

He could feel the individual beads of sweat rolling down his neck. He glanced over at the young woman next to him. She was full into her workout now, going into sprints for 1-2 minutes at a time, then slowing her pace down to a continuous jog.

Nothing. She didn't even look over at me when I looked her way.

Tobias set the pace on his treadmill a little faster so he could break a real sweat. He turned up his own music, the fat beats pumping him up even further. Another five minutes go by and Tobias can feel the sweat begin to bead up on his arms and the back of his neck, sweat rolling down his back and collecting at the bottom of his shirt. He glanced over at the young jogger beside him.

Still nothing. She didn't even look my way. She's unfazed by the pill! This is bull!

He put another five minutes of continuous running, breaking his 2-mile pace and moving into his third mile, almost to his fourth, then he looked over at her.

She had just hit the cool down button on her workout, her body covered in a layer of sweat. Some more strands of her hair had come down around her face and at the back of her neck, her breathing a little labored. Their eyes made contact.

And that's when Tobias saw it; the same gloss over the eyes that Betty had the night before. The blond jogger averted her eyes in another moment and hit the stop button on her machine, grabbing her keys and water bottle from the cup holders. Then she his Tobias' stop button as well.

Oh, shit.

"Can you come here for a second?"

Tobias was a bit out of breath but managed an, "Okay," and grabbed his own set of keys and water bottle, walking back past the cardio machines, past the weights and his mother who was completely distracted by her trainer, and back to the lockers, the young jogger walking into one of the uni-sex changing rooms. She pulled Tobias in by his sweaty shirt.

It's working! It's fucking working! Tobias' heart was beating a thousand beats a minute at what things she had in store for him.

"I don't know what it is," she started, "but I haven't been able to stop thinking about you since you got on the treadmill next to me. And that's not like me. I'm not like this." She seemed almost apologetic.

"Like what?" Tobias questioned, wiping the sweat from his forehead with his towel.

The jogger locked the door behind her.

"Like this." He felt one of her hands pull him to her and her lips were on his in an instant, full of passion and lust, her body pressed against his. She was searching for something to do with her hands, her fingers running across his back, clawing at his chest when, suddenly, they found their place. She pulled his shorts down around his ankles.

Oh, shit!

Episode Six:

Recoil

Oh, shit was right! Tobias and the young jogger pressed one another's flesh for some time in the changing room until she became vocal once he was inside her. Once that happened, he knew that being caught fucking in the gym wouldn't be that good of a plan if he wanted his experiments to remain secret.

My pill-popping days would be over after the first real try, Tobias reminded himself, covering her mouth with his own, her hands grabbing at his hair as she rode him on the changing bench.

"What's your name?" She looked at him with eyes still glazed over, her strong calves wrapped around his waist. The more she pulled closer to him, the deeper he could feel himself being pushed inside of her.

"Tobias."

"Tobias, this feels so good!"

"What's yours?"

"Sadie." He saw her eyes close then, her stifled moans beginning to spread once she closed the world out around her. Even the overhead speaker that pumped out motivational workout music wouldn't be able to drown out the pleasure noises she would make if he continued.

So, the showers were his best bet. Both the male and female showers were separate, but each shower had an individual stall that you could go into and have privacy. He had to get her in the male shower room.

"I want to shower with you, Sadie."

And that was all that was needed. Sadie was so compliant that she slowed her pace, though he could see in her face that she didn't want to, and let him leave, going to check out the showers.

Presently, there was no one in there, which worked to Tobias' advantage. He grabbed two of the complimentary shower towels and picked the handicap stall that contained the pull down shower bench. No sooner had he turned around that Sadie was there. The look in her eyes silenced any protests that he may have made at that moment. And that fact that she had already taken off her clothes and was upon him kind of sealed the deal as well.

"I couldn't wait that long, Tobias. We need to continue."

And continue they did. After the handicap stall door was shut and the lock on the door slid to the side, Tobias got the full measure of Sadie's thighs around him, biting down on his neck as she came over and over again, the hot water washing away the sweat and the sex at the same time.

As Tobias and Sadie came in unison, the water dripping over their shaking forms, Tobias thought of one thing: *one pill, good sex. Two pills, fucking mind-blowing sex.*

Sadie slowed her pace and rested on Tobias' thighs, his arms pulling her close. He kissed her, she melted. They melted together. It was what he wanted, what he needed. Sadie ran her fingers through his hair, her body quivering from the pleasure.

*　　　　*　　　　*

But, at some point, Tobias had to return to the real world. He couldn't just be fucking and coming all the time, now could he? No, of course not. (*Those that said yes, bite me.*)

The Avengers buzz continued for the next few days, with Tobias and his friends going to see the movie two more times together, trying their best to find the easter eggs within the film and pick apart the movie for any inaccuracies. Joss Whedon had done a great job. Fan-Dome had a burst of new readers after the blockbuster film and Tobias enjoyed working a few extra hours to keep things on the walls and endcaps stocked up.

Besides, he needed the money to save up for college once he left at the end of the summer. A week had passed since getting the Pill and Tobias felt like things were beginning to get back to normal. However, he still had reoccurring visions of the two women and their excellent body parts all over him, sending him into sudden erection mode, doing his best to find a safe place until the moment subsided.

Forty-seven pills left. Now what to do with them? Tobias had made a list of scenarios in a week's time and was playing it safe at the moment, doing his best to think out his plan before just acting as he had done the first two times. He didn't really count Betty Boop. *That was more of a trial and error moment*, he concluded, *but Sadie definitely wasn't an accident.*

New Comic book Wednesdays were always a ritual of sorts for Tobias and the crew he hung out with. Before he graduated high school, he would ride the bus home from school and sit with his friends in the back of the gaming room, reading the comics from his hold box for 2-3 hours at a time, debating what was going to happen in the story or which was the best ongoing storyline. It was good to be able to talk about things he was interested in with fellow nerds; there weren't many places he could do this and feel comfortable without feeling like he was a geek. He was. They were. But they were in their own sanctuary.

However, on this particular day, even sanctuary couldn't save a nerd.

110

When Douglas came in to get the morning deposits as he always did, the whole crew was a little bit surprised to see him stay more than just a moment.

"Since when did you graduate from being a geek to a real person, Tobes?" But Tobias didn't get a chance to answer. Being in the process of buying a soda and a small bag of Doritos at the checkout, he was caught off guard at Douglas' assault, which started with a hard push up against the snack rack, an assortment of candy bars and potato chip bags scattering across the floor by his feet.

His younger brother Mark protested on the other side of the counter.

"Hey, bro, what are you doing?"

However, his complaint stopped before it really got a chance to start any further, the look in his brother's eyes enough to unveil the true coward that mark had always been.

Douglas didn't even look in his brother's direction after that, his anger focused on the cowering Tobias who did his best not to slip on slip on the chip bags at his feet.

"Hey, Doug. I'm sure there's been some kind of misunderstanding!"

Clark chimed in. "Yeah, Tobias just graduated from high school, but he's totally a geek. In fact, we-" he trailed off when he saw Douglas clench his fists at his side.

"Tobias!" But it was too late. Doug's anger had been unleashed. Douglas belted the quivering geek in front of him, knocking him back into the rack completely, dropping him to the ground.

Tobias' jaw exploded in pain. It felt as if that entire side of his face had been stung by hundreds of bees all at once.

Nevertheless, that didn't stop Doug from continuing.

112

"'He's a real man! He kept me company. I've never felt like that before in my life!' Is that it, Tobester?"

Doug hefted the nerd up easily into his grip, his muscles bulging underneath the tight black tee he wore. Mark's older brother tossed Tobias further into the store, the nerd dropping his Mountain Dew and Doritos as he collided with the vintage toy aisle. Episode I Star Wars carded figures rained down upon him. He tried his best to get up but his head was still ringing from that first punch. Tobias thought he heard his friends calling out to him again. He turned to look in their direction when another of Doug's punches sent him reeling to the floor.

Betty. Pretty, loud, sexy Betty Boop. Her ass alone should be made into a sculpture and be chiseled from the most costly marble. Even now, thinking of that moment, Tobias smiled through the pain. In the few seconds that Tobias had to think, he asked himself if it had been worth it, if having that stranger ride him and show him what good sexy really felt like was worth the epic beating he was getting now.

And the answer that swirled through his mind was always the same; a resounding yes.

"You thinks its funny, you little piece of shit?"

Tobias heard his friend's protestations in the background but it was all garbled voices, like that of Charlie Brown's teacher.

Wa Wa, Wa Wa Wa Wa Wa.

Doug grabbed him up from the floor and jerked him up by the Yellow Lantern shirt he wore, which was ripped and covered with spots of red on it.

My blood. I'm bleeding. And I bought this shirt here when it first came out! Fitting.

His mind was reeling. His body felt as light as a feather and as hard as bricks at the same time, which he didn't even know was possible.

And then something within Tobias struck out. Deep inside the geek that had never been in a fight before but had been bullied plenty throughout his middle school and high school years, something stirred and came to life.

And his body responded immediately. His hand instinctively smacked Doug's hands away, freeing himself from his attacker's hold. And his right hand...

...that glorious hand that had been creator of sketches, doer of homework, button-pushing co-pilot with the left hand on all video games, and even girlfriend and fantasy pin-up girl under the covers on those late and lonely nights, fought back.

It curled his fingers into a ball and launched itself at Doug with full force, slamming into the man's left temple. Tobias had just fought back.

Doug fell back for a second, covering his left eye, looking at Tobias in disbelief that he had been struck.

Tobias looked at his fighting right hand, smiled, then looked at his friends, all whose faces were cringed in sympathetic pain and surprise. He followed all of their gazes- and met Doug's fist one last time before flying off his feet and into unconsciousness.

Episode Seven:

Nursing Wounds of War

'I had met Mark at the comic store. I had never been to one without my dad; didn't know much about comics really, but had found myself sitting in the car in front of the newly-designed, newly-renovated comic book store across town; the only one that we could find that would take comics; Fan-Dome Comics and Collectibles. It was a new neon sign then, not faded with time and the wear and tear of the environment.

"Go on, son. Go ahead and take them in and see what they say. I'll be in there in a minute."

Mom still looked tired. It had been months since her last chemotherapy session.

The packing and the moving and the stress of it all must be getting to her.

The comic book store looked so small on the outside but, once you walked in and that little motion bell rang for the employees, a whole world opened up. Action figures, comics, movies, T-shirts, backpacks; everything a kid could possibly want that had to do with superheroes was here. My eyes shifted and wandered to all of the aisles before me, in awe at how much of an empire that comic books had made.

But I didn't want to get distracted from my mission, couldn't get distracted. I sat the box down on the floor next to the counter, leaning on the counter, waiting for someone to help. Some kid a few years older than me rose from behind the counter, a faded Ghost Rider shirt on his thick form.

"What can I help you with today, dude?" But he didn't have time to answer. From a few aisles away, a fresh grown up emerged, a then 20-year-old Douglas, sporting a fresh haircut and a Fan-Dome polo shirt with the logo embroidered on the left side.

"Shut up, Mark!"

"I was just trying to help!"

"You know what dad says about being behind the counter when there are customers!"

The younger kid sulked for a second and then walked out from around the counter, disappearing into an aisle not far away.

"What can I help you with, kid?"

"I have some comics to sell."

"Are you eighteen?"

"No, I'm thirteen."

"You have to be eighteen or have a parent with you."

"My mom's in the car."

"Okay. That'll work. Let me take a look at what you got and you can go get your mom for me. Cool?"

"Cool."

An hour after browsing through the store and finding a ton of things I'd love to have, the store clerk named Douglas called us over.

"It looks like there's quite a bit of wear on the edges and the spines aren't up to par enough to be considered mint. But, for the most part, you have a pretty nice collection. You only have about two hundred comics but the ones you do have got a nice price tag on them. Whoever collected these knew what they were doing." That's when Mom piped in.

"It was his father's collection. He was a big collector of comics and stuff like that."

"Well, I can pay you $3,000 dollars for what you have here. Do you take checks? I'm afraid we don't have that much cash in the store right now."

Three thousand dollars! I had to blink several times and pinch myself to make sure it wasn't a dream.

Money was money and I was out to get as much as I could for the hidden treasure I had found left by my dad.

It was the least he could do, I thought to myself, having looked at the amount of bills he had left behind for mom to take care of all by herself.

"What about the story?"

"The story?"

"Yeah, is the story any good?" I pointed at the cover with Spiderman spinning a web at the Green Goblin.

"It doesn't matter anymore, kid. It's priced based upon whether or not it's a classic. We just go by the pricing guide we have." Douglas lifted up the pricing guide he had used to price each comic.

This was no library; the employees here did not read the contents within the room, the scattered selection of Marvel, DC, and other independent comics that sat on the shelves just behind them and all around them.

"Well, it should be."

It was then that I knew that I loved comics. No, that I **would love** comics. They had been neglected, misused, discarded by most of society. I would do everything I could to nurse them back to health.

*   *   *

Tobias blinked himself awake.

100 24pt Virgin White Boards by ComiCare. Resealable Polypropylene Comic Book Bags.

Is this what my life has been reduced to?

Tobias stared at the back stock of comic boards and bags as they came into view through his blurred

122

vision, listening to the others around him in a hushed tone wait for him to come back to the world of the living. The first voice he heard belonged to Clark, the concern in his tone coming out without caring about what the others thought around them.

"Are you alright, Tobias? You took a pretty bad spill."

"Yeah, a spill through all the vintage figures section! How am I going to explain this to dad? He won't—" And then Mark became the asshole again.

But the others stopped him before he could start.

"Would you shut the hell up, Mark! If all of us need to chip in to pay for the damages, we will. We need to find out if Tobias is going to be okay first!"

And Mark's moment of complaint had been stifled, at least for the moment.

Junior piped in this time, his analytical analysis of the situation coming out, as though he had days to think on it and not just a few minutes while Tobias had been unconscious.

"Maybe your brother should pay for the damages. After all, he was the one that started the whole thing in the first place. You've got the security footage, too. You're lucky that Tobias is a friend of yours. Any other customer would have your ass in court for not calling the cops."

"Shut the fuck up, guys, we need to see how Tobias is!" Suddenly, Mark was on board with the Tobias train of concern.

"Hey, Tobias. You alright, little buddy?" This whole thing for Tobias felt like a very strange episode of Gilligan's Island. He always felt like Gilligan and never any other character in his life. Well, not until now.

Tobias had gone for so long living through the adventures Peter Parker and Mary Jane would go through on the pages of the books, always looking for
124

some further meaning behind it all. Tobias knew that, someday, he would get his chance.

But is this what my chance looks like? Mark brought over the comic book bag full of ice from the fridge in the break room and handed it to Travis, letting him put it on the fresh bruises that Mark's older brother had made.

"You really pulled a George McFly back there, Tobias." Mark even went so far as to recreate the scene in the comic book stock room. "'Hey you, get your damn hands off her!'"

"Yeah, but I wasn't fighting for my mother's virginity."

Clark countered. "It looks like you were fighting for your own virginity. What an ass whooping you took, Tobias! What did you do to piss him off?"

Fuck one of his girls. That's what Tobias wanted to say. But instead, it was, "I think I disrespected his girl the other night."

"Yeah, by being inside her!" Mark chuckled at the thought. He scratched at the small amount of facial hair that he had, still checking outside in the comic shop for his brother.

"I don't think he's coming back anytime soon, guys. I'll go flip the sign to closed on the door and be right back." Clark stared in disbelief at what he had just heard. He looked over at Tobias with wide eyes.

"Is Mark telling the truth? Did you have sex with one of his women?"

Tobias nodded, still in pain. Junior was dumbfounded. Clark, on the other hand, needed more information.

"Were you the aggressor in this sexual act?" Clark looked dead serious when he asked it. And Tobias could tell that this conversation wasn't about Doug and the Battle Royale that just took place in the comic store. It was about having intercourse with a woman. And Clark desperately wanted more

126

information. In fact, there was hope in his voice that it was all true.

Mark came back and pointed to the beaten and bruised Tobias.

"Do you really think that he was the aggressor?"

Clark countered and turned the questioning to Mark.

"And how do you know about this?"

"I just put it together now. Last night, Doug was having an argument over the phone with one of his girls. He was pretty mad. And, when he came in and started something with Tobias, I just figured it out. Tobias had something to do with that conversation last night.

Tobias tried to play it off. "I guess she thought I was somebody else. I don't know. I just went with it."

Clark nodded, still transfixed on what Tobias was saying. "I think all of us would have done the same."

Junior piped up just then, scaring all of them in the stock room.

"I knew it! You wouldn't dare miss the first few minutes of the most epic superhero movie of all time without good reason. And I knew that line you used about the concession stand being busy was bogus!" Junior gave himself a high five, practically ecstatic with inappropriate giggles. He caught himself in another few seconds and reeled it back.

"You got me, dead to rights, Junior."

When Mark left the stockroom again, the two of them moved closer to Tobias, handing him more ice, a plush Totoro to put behind his head, and a bottle of water. But they all weren't thinking about Tobias' recovery. And, as they spoke in unison, Tobias knew he couldn't just leave the story as it was.

"What was it like?"

Tobias couldn't leave them hanging. He had to tell them something. He told them about Maggie; he told them everything **except** about the pill. He even added how she had been interested in him the other night when they met upstairs, which was a complete lie but made the story more believable.

*   *   *

Tobias had to make up a lie to his Mom or he would never be able to go back to the comic store again. He sat on the roof of their apartment complex that night, watching for her car, when Mark pulled up in his lot. Tobias had an ice pack on his eye and had already put some ointment on his scrapes and small nicks, looking as though he got in a fight with a cat and not a grown man.

He motioned to Mark and his friend nodded, coming up through the stairwell and was soon on the top of the roof with him, climbing out onto the four-story roof that overlooked the entire complex.

"What are you doing up here?"

"I feel like Batman when I'm up here."

"Well, you feel like flying high, Batman?" Mark pulled out a bag of weed, his small metal pipe and a lighter, sitting on the roof next to Tobias.

"Apology weed, my man; straight from my brother's stash. He totally doesn't know I have it. I'd get my ass beat if he knew." He paused, placing a little bit of the weed in the end of the pipe.

"Tobias, I really am sorry about my brother's bullshit that he pulled today. I talked to my Dad and he says name your price, as long as you don't press charges." That and many other things Mark said to Tobias. If anything, this was Tobias' chance to get things that he wanted. He could have the store closed down and lawyers all over Mark's brother and father for the shit that was pulled earlier today.

Tobias settled for his hold box being picked up for the next two months and a set of the new

130

Batman: Arkham City collector's figures that had just come out a few months back. They were sitting on the shelf at the store. He shook Mark's hand. By the end of that week, they were displayed on Tobias' shelf in his room.

They passed the peace pipe for a time in silence. Then Tobias started his theories.

"What if I was Batman? Wouldn't that be awesome? To be Batman?" Tobias and Mark sat out on the tilted 4th floor roof of his apartment, looking up at the stars. It was around midnight or so. His mom still hadn't come home.

Maybe she's working late. In another moment, he checked his phone and saw a message from her that confirmed what he had been thinking.

"You'd never get any ass, that's for sure."

"Why do you say that?"

"Because of that suit, man. Think of how hard it would be to take off. It would take forever to have sex with someone; and then the smell from wearing it all the time- and the chaffing. Jesus, just the chaffing would be painful!"

"Good point. No one talks about that when Batman suits up. He doesn't put on any Gold Bond or jock itch powder. I'm pretty sure his suits stink after fighting crime all night." Tobias agreed, passing the small silver pipe with a lighter back to Mark. He took a hit from it and let it sink in for a moment, looking at the stars up above them.

"I'm sure that's what the pressurized chamber is for that we always see. He doesn't want to smell that shit while he's in the Batcave."

That started a laughing fit out of Tobias who, in turn, came back with another thought.

"'Dammit, Alfred! What the fuck is that smell? Did you die in here or something?' That's some type of shit I could see Batman saying."

"No, Tobias! It would be like Batman blaming Alfred like he was a dog. 'Damn, Alfred! What have you been eating down in the Batcave, tacos?'"

Both of them were laughing now, letting the humor of Batman's private life rattle through their high minds.

"So, how did it happen, man? I never got the story." Tobias knew it would be only a matter of time before Mark would ask how he got himself laid.

And, soon, he'll be asking for help getting him some as well. But there were more pressing matters at hand.

"What am I going to tell my mom, Mark? She's going to see right through me."

Mark took a hit from the pipe and thought for a moment, passing the pipe back to Tobias.

"I would tell her the truth, just say it happened somewhere else besides the comic shop. Hell, I'll back you up and say my brother was being a dick."

Just then, Tobias could see his mother pulling up in the parking lot just below them. She didn't seem them on the roof as she went inside.

Mark blew out the last of the smoke and popped a mint in his mouth, putting away his contraband so Tobias' mother wouldn't smell it. He pulled out a can of Axe spray and doused the both of them before they walked back into the hallway.

"Hey, just food for thought, Tobias. You might think about fucking someone that's not seeing a total asshole on the side, okay? And, hey, you could always date an older woman. You know, a cougar. I hear they like'em young."

A cougar, huh? I'm not totally opposed to that, Tobias decided, still high as a kite yet still trying to stay grounded. But the intrigue of being with an older woman was beginning to churn around in his mind.

What have I started?

134

Episode Eight:

Research Through the Ages

"Do you like it when I move like that?" Tobias watched with amazement at the woman hovering over him, her breasts pressing against his chest, her hands interlocked in his own, holding him down on her bed. She moved her hips again, sliding slowly down the pulsing member jutting out from between his legs. The young man's eyes nearly rolled back into his head, the heels of his feet digging into the mattress to keep her from repeating that motion again.

She's going to make me come, Tobias' mind screamed, but she didn't seem to care in the least, tilting her hips again, Tobias' load erupting inside her seconds later, the woman milking him dry with her own throbbing sex. She watched him writhe under her, his hands still raised over his head and spread out on both sides.

*   *   *

Her name was Angela. She was a woman he found at a local bar, very upper class place. *At least, that's what the ad in the paper said,* Tobias concluded, looking around at the clientele that filled the bar and even some of the booths at the place. He had the taxi drop him off three blocks away from the bar so he could jog the rest of the way there and break a good sweat before walking in. He didn't have much to wear in regards to fashion, so he just wore his church clothes without the formal tie, letting the two buttons down on the dress shirt so he could look at least half normal.

The pill did the rest for him. He didn't know what old or too old was, so he just looked for someone that he could picture naked and having fun with him, something he was sure would occur now that he had the pill. *It was a sure thing every time*, the young man assured himself, *so pick out whomever you like.*

Tobias did just that, looking at the busty brunette at the corner of the bar. She was sipping on something in a martini glass and didn't pay him any mind at all; until he sat down next to her. He gave the effects of the pill a few minutes to work and then made eye contact with her.

"Where did you come from, you adorable little thing?" Tobias smiled at her.

"What's your name, pretty lady?" He was still warming up when it came to pick up lines.

But why do I need pick up lines when I have the pill to do the work for me?

*   *   *

"You knew I was coming. Why didn't you stop? Tobias, though still caught in the pleasure from the act, seemed a little upset. She smiled at him. It was a delicious smile that told him quite a bit. First, it told him that he didn't know shit about sex, but it was in a playful, very disarming way. After all, she was completely naked on top of him, his pleasured member still inside of her. She had a light layer of sweat on her brow from the exertion but she still seemed quite able to go as long as she wanted to, sliding off of Tobias' small frame to let him recover.

"What do you mean? I enjoy pleasing you. You should hear yourself. It's quite the earful. Very much a turn-on." Tobias didn't know if that was the pill talking or Angela herself. It was beginning to be hard to tell the difference, for he hadn't seen any woman in their natural form prior to the pill with the

138

exception of them being completely disinterested in him from the get go.

Am I such a bad person, he wondered. *I'm not ugly, I'm not fat. I shower and keep myself looking presentable. I have goals that are attainable; I'm loyal and faithful when I'm in a relationship.*

Angela must have caught him deep in thought while still being inside her, for she began to move her hips in that oh-so-perfect way, getting his attention, as well as the attention of a close friend of his.

"There he is. Oh, I knew he'd be back. He just needed to get that first one out of his system. Now he's ready for more."

"He is?" Tobias had no idea if he'd be ready for more or not.

"Yes. He's now ready for Angela. The real question is-" The older woman moved closer, her warm body lighting up his cooled skin, her breath raspy in his ear as she spoke. "-are you ready for me,

Tobias?" He answered her the only way that he knew how to, with a kiss; a deep, hot, passionate kiss that sent his insides to churning and bringing rigidity back to his cock inside of her, awakening her wet flower as well. She smiled at him through the kiss.

"I guess I got my answer."

Tobias woke that morning to the smell of bacon and eggs. Multiple parts of his body were sore but they didn't dare complain to him because the young man was still in a state of bliss. Every part of him had aches and pains but, as he sat up and pressed a pillow underneath his chest, he had never felt this good in his entire life.

His stomach growled to life as soon as he smelled the food cooking downstairs. Tobias looked for his clothes and found a robe laid out at the edge of the bed by his feet. It was a man's robe. He slipped out of bed and slipped it on, tying it around the waist, making his way out of the bedroom.

In the daylight, the house was quite striking. Everything had its place. It was very organized and very full of color; pastels and stronger colors lines the hallway past the other rooms, then the living room opened up before him and it was nothing but a great glass wall looking out over the city. Tobias turned and saw Angela in the kitchen, her back to him. He turned back to beautiful view, taking a few steps down into the step down living room.

The living room seemed to be made for this view, Tobias remarked, his feet a little cold against the white marble of the floors. He stepped onto a rug underneath the coffee table to warm them up. He noticed then why he hadn't noticed the glass wall the night before; there were a great set of shades that were controlled by a panel on the wall that opened and closed them whenever it was needed.

He heard Angela clanking around in the kitchen then so he turned his attention back to her, still reeling from such a great view from where they were.

"You have a really nice place here. I love the view."

Angela sat two plates down in front of them on the dining room table that was adjacent to the kitchen. She didn't have a smile on her face. In fact, Tobias noticed that she didn't seem happy to see him.

Uh-oh, the pill has worn off! What Angela said next only confirmed what he was thinking.

"Why are you here, Tobias?"

"I'm sorry, Angela. Did you not want me here?"

"Don't turn things around. What are you doing here, Tobias? We don't know each other, I'm 41 and you're 18, or at least that's what it says on your driver's license." Angela tossed his wallet onto the dining room table. She pointed over at the couch where his clothes lay folded for him.

142

"I'm sorry. I didn't mean to make things weird."

She smiled but it was a serious smile. It looked as though she really didn't want to deal with any bullshit.

"I must have gotten hammered last night, because I don't remember bringing you home with me."

"Oh."

Angela suddenly seemed somewhat apologetic.

"Not that you're not great, young man, it's just that I don't know what came over me. It was something that you said or did that reeled me in. I just wanted you. That was it. And it was really good, I do remember that."

Tobias was beaming as he ate at his eggs and bacon. The robe was really comfortable but his feet were getting cold. He moved to his clothes on the couch and noticed that they had been washed and dried and folded. He slipped on his socks and returned to the table, pouring himself some orange juice from the carafe that was sitting out.

"Well, at least that's a plus, huh?"

"Very much a plus." She took a drink of her coffee.

"I'm sorry. Where are my manners? Would you like some coffee, Tobias?"

Tobias nodded. "Yes, thank you."

Angela got up from her chair and grabbed him a cup from the cupboard, pouring him a cup. She sat it down next to his place.

"Thank you."

"So, did you drug me or something?" Tobias almost spit out the fresh coffee when she asked that.

"Is that how it works now? I don't really do this, you know, pick up women or get picked up by women."

"Some people are desperate like that. I've never been caught in that kind of snare before. But I've heard of people having that happen to them. It's not a nice world out there."

144

Tobias hated to lie to Angela but she wouldn't understand the dynamics and Tobias didn't feel like his game being up just because he wanted to sleep with a cougar once.... well twice last night.

"I'm here because I'm awful at sex. I haven't had any good sex before."

"Well, you weren't awful last night. You could work on it but I've seen much worse, Tobias. You're far from awful."

"That's good to know."

"Well, are you saying you need some practice, Tobias?"

"I'm always up for practice."

Angela smiled. It was that same smile from last night that caused so much trouble. She moved in closer to him, reaching underneath his bathrobe for his cock, which was already ahead of the game.

"Oh, you want some real practice with an erection like that."

And that's when Tobias received his first blowjob. He had to put down his coffee it was so good. He didn't bother to stop Angela or direct her in any way. She knew exactly what she was doing.

You were absolutely right, Mark. It was worth a try. A very good, hard, stiff, wet try that was about to happen again.

Episode Nine:

Intimacy 101

Tobias spent most of the morning at Angela's and a good part of the afternoon in her bed for recovery from the morning and the previous evening.

With his mom working during the mornings, he had the time available to go out and hang out with friends or use the pill when he wanted, which had been quite a bit in the last few days since he had it.

His friends were surprised to see him at new comic Wednesday when he finally arrived.

"Hey, guys. How's it going?" Mark nodded and went back to the register when a customer approached the counter. Clark and Junior are sitting at their usual place at the gaming tables.

Clark nods his hello and continues to read his hold box comics for this week. He points with his nose at the stack of comics sitting at Tobias' spot. They're Tobias' comics. *They kept my place.*

Tobias takes his place and gets to reading his first comic of the day; Detective Comics.

Nothing kicks more ass than Batman!

Then to another; Batman. Then he takes a detour and moves to a Marvel title; Iron Man. In another few minutes, he gets a Mountain Dew and a bag of chips. While he's at the checkout, he sees a stack of club flyers on the counter. He picks one up.

"Hey, Mark. What's this?" He turns it over and sees the talent line-up on the back.

"It's my penance for saying shit to that Goth chick the other day. She complained to my dad and he complied by allowing her to distribute this shit at his store. It's some new club that ravers go to. There's some line-up of bands this whole week. Shit actually looks pretty dope." Mark chuckled. "Tobias, you actually thinking about going? I don't think this is much of your thing."

"Yeah, you're probably right. Could be a mosh pit or something. Then I'd get tore up."

"Damn straight you would!" Mark grabbed his stack of comics and went to sit down at the table with them.

Hell yes, I'm fucking going to this! This was one of the scenarios on his list! In fact, it was in the top five! It was only a five-dollar cover and it was eighteen and up, which made it perfect for him.

I wonder what three pills would do? Tobias could only imagine.

He spent the rest of the afternoon there with his friends, helping out with the comic duties as he always did, having the discussions that he knew that he would miss once he got to college. *This is my last summer here,* he reminded himself, knowing that he wouldn't be seeing several of his friends until Christmas break or Spring break once college started.

It wasn't as if I was going to a college nearby. Tobias had accepted a scholarship at Stratton University, an art college three hours away from where he was now, which meant that he wouldn't be commuting back and forth in Bolingbrook.

His life was changing by the second and there was nothing that he could do about it. He knew that this was the case so he rolled with the punches. But, with the pill, at least it was tolerable.

He smiled at the thought of the future, mainly because it involved naked, moaning, completely desirous of him women. And that's never a bad thing.

150

As soon as Tobias got to the club, he looked for the first hot female bartender. He had made it a point to have the taxi stop him half a mile away from the club just so he could break a sweat before he got there, to give time for the pills to take effect.

Forty-two left. He had taken three pills just an hour ago, so he let them have some time to take effect. After all, he had never been to a club before, so he didn't know if he would like it and didn't want to stay in it any longer than he had to.

Going into uncharted territory for the umpteenth time now, Tobias reminded himself. This pill had definitely expanded his horizons in numerous ways in the short amount of time having it.

After seeing it from the outside, Tobias knew exactly where he was. The club had been an old firehouse that was condemned years earlier after the relocation and creation of a new firehouse closer to the middle of town. This place looked like the

Ghostbusters building, complete with the Ghostbusters sign attached to the side of the building. But this sign was a bit different. Instead of a ghost on the sign, there was a DJ and his DJ table, a thick pair of sunglasses on the DJ's face that covered up most of his features.

The Rec Room was it's name. Next experiment; three pills in public.

The club was packed. And it had good reason to be, too. It was only the fourth day of being opened and each floor of the renovated firehouse looked spotless. Black lights, fog machines, strobe lights, massive speakers; you couldn't ask for more from a club. That and the fact that they had the old go-go dancer cages at the corners of each stage so women could dance in them was pretty spectacular, too, Tobias decided, taking it all in as he stood at the bar.

He knew that the stamp on his hand would give him away to the bartender but he had to try. He braved
152

the storm and turned around to the bartender. She was a short, sexy brunette that wore a Catholic school girl outfit, filling it out in the top and bottom with a tanned set of breasts that nearly popped out of her sports bra and tanned thighs that could barely be seen because of the thigh highs she wore.

She looked at the stamp on his hand and then at Tobias, who definitely couldn't pass for twenty-one, even if he had grown a moustache and had chest hair bursting out of his button down shirt. Presently, he had seven chest hairs.

Then her voice surprised him.

"What can I get you, sexy?" He looked into her eyes. They were glazed over, just like the others before her.

It works! It actually works! I can't believe this!

Tobias was so caught up with that fact that he forgot that she was asking for his drink of choice.

Just say something, dammit! Something you've heard people drink before.

"Jack and coke, please!"

"Sure thing." She didn't take her eyes off him, with the exception to mix the jack and coke together. She sat the drink on the counter and waited for him to reach for it. When he did, placing a ten-dollar bill on the counter, she pushed it away, running her fingers down the length of his own.

"It's on me, tiger. I get off in a few hours if you'd like to have some more drinks."

"Thanks." *How did he respond to that?* But Tobias didn't have time to respond. Another woman standing next to him turned to him and smiled. She was dressed in a skin-tight little tiger print dress, her hair teased up around her face, her shapely form moving closer to him. Tobias tasted the drink.

Most awful drink ever! Tasted like burn licorice dipped in soda! He downed it immediately. *Whoever said I had to like it?*

"Hey there! Please say you have the time because I definitely do, too!" Tobias had never been hit on but he was surprised at the amount of cheesy lines that women would deliver in order to get with a guy. He sat the empty glass down on the counter behind him and began to move away from the bar.

"No thanks. I'm here with someone."

"She can join in, too, if you like."

"No thank you."

What is going on with these people? Is everyone secretly horny all the time, they just don't say it?

Tobias moved through the crowd as quick as he could, making his way to the bathroom so he could wash off the light layer of sweat that had started to accumulate on his body.

I think three pills is a bit too much. Let's just say this experiment is over for tonight.

Tobias didn't want to take chances like this. He was a very safe person. He had never taken risks before, let alone with his life and other peoples. This situation was beginning to be a bit intense.

He washed off the sweat and cleaned his neck and hairline with wet paper towels, drying off the best he could. The concierge in the bathroom just looked at him like he was on crack.

"I'm a heavy sweater."

"I can see that."

Tobias walked back out into the club and made for the exit, the band onstage in full effect, the crowd thicker than it had been before. He looked for a way out. And that's when he saw her.

It was Cassidy, the Goth Chick, and she saw him immediately. There was a slight smile at the corner of her mouth. That's all she gave him. He made his way over to her.

"Hi."

She looked at him, still rocking to the music, her eyes intent on the band.

"Hi."

"I saw the flyers at the comic shop, decided I'd try it out."

"That's cool that you came. Not many people at Fan-Dome would do that."

Tobias didn't have a chance to get another word in. Behind him, the bartender had showed up, a jack and coke in each hand.

"Hey, sexy! So this is where you wandered off too, huh?"

She handed him the drink and took a drink of her own, grabbing at his neck with her free hand. She kissed him hard, pushing some of her own drink in his mouth. He swallowed it down, some of it dribbling down his chin. She licked it off for him.

"What do you say we ditch this place and find a nice, quiet place?" Tobias took a drink of his own jack and coke, the burnt licorice taste coming back to his palate. He looked over to Cassidy apologetically.

She just smiled a bit more. That's when he saw tiger print tight skirt approaching, drinks in hand. And she was eyeballing him hard, but eyeballing the bartender with him even harder.

Oh, shit! Tobias had to do something. He really didn't want to find out what could potentially happen right now. He wasn't up for was these three pills were putting down. He downed his drink and handed it to the bartender.

"Can you get me another, sweetie?"

"Sure thing. Then can we get out of here?"

"Whatever you say." She laid a hard kiss on his mouth and moved back through the crowd, the other woman approaching closer and closer.

Tobias turned to Cassidy, a look of panic on his face.

"I know this is a bit strange but I need your help."

Cassidy turned her attention away from the stage to Tobias.

"What's up?"

"Can I get a ride home. You see, that's my ex-girlfriend and she's a bit psycho."

"I can see that."

"When she comes back, I think things are going to get out of hand. It always happens when she starts drinking."

"Shit. That must be a lot due to the fact that she's a bartender."

"I know, right!"

Cassidy took another few nods to the music and then answered.

"Sure, my rides just outside. Right now?"

"If that's not too much trouble."

She shook her head and then began weaving through the crowd.   Tobias followed, narrowly escaping the tiger print hottie.

As soon as he got outside, he took a breath of fresh air. It felt the like the first breathe of air during winter and his lungs thanked him gratefully.

"My car's just right over there. Hey, where do you live anyway?"

"Not far. Just like 15 minutes away." She nodded again in understanding. He climbed into her car and closed the door behind him. She started it up and was about to pull out when Tobias could see the bartender walking out of the bar with drinks in her hands.

"Oh, shit! There she is!" He ducked down in the car as they drove through the parking lot and out onto the main street.

Once they were away safely, Tobias sat back up in the seat, leaning back, closing his eyes.

"That was close."

"Another minute and she would've been having you for a late night snack, I believe. Look at Tobias, the stud!" He could hear the sarcasm in her voice. "Who would have thought? All those years, quiet in high school, sitting in the comic book store with his nerd buddies." She laughed at his situation.

"Yeah, who would have thought it?"

"Maybe the club is not your type of place, Tobias."

"Yeah, that's what Mark said earlier."

"Yeah, well Mark's an asshole!"

"Yes, Cassidy. Yes, he is."

Cassidy pulled up to his apartment complex several minutes later. They sat in the car in silence for a moment, Tobias taking a breather from what just happened.

That was too close! And the lies were getting more frequent. A crazy ex-girlfriend? Who would believe that?

Then Cassidy's voice broke the silence.

"I listened to your arguments at the comic store, Tobias. All the time I knew you were right, had been right, for some time. You're talented. You've got a good mind for storytelling."

"Thank you. I appreciate that. That means a lot coming from you."

Tobias wiped the sweat from his forehead and wiped it off on his jeans.

Sweat? Cassidy. The pill. Confined space. Uh-oh!

But it was too late. Cassidy already had that look in her eyes, the same look the other women had, except this time, she was already upon him. Her

162

mouth was on him, her hands grabbing for the button to undo his jeans. The pill had a hold on her.

"What are you doing, Cassidy?"

"I don't know. I can't help it! I think I'm going to fuck you right now!"

In some worlds, in some cultures even, men are threatened by an over-dominant woman who takes control in the bedroom.

But this wasn't a bedroom, Tobias reminded himself, this was a piece of junk car. *And this wasn't simply a woman.* Cassidy had been untouchable among all of his friends since day one of her coming into the comic book store for her brooding and more often times than not, melancholy comics.

She was soft, much softer than she looked. The smile underneath the piercings had always been so standoffish. But now, in her car, an old Dodge Dart that smelled of years of her father's cigar smoke, the smile was disarming and inviting at the same time.

The corset she wore underneath the vintage rocker tee was unlaced and tossed out the window onto the empty street. The black, sheer undershirt came off as well but the plethora of necklaces remained, the cold metal pressing against Tobias' barren and sweaty chest.

I don't care if it's the pill taking effect on her! I want this more than anything now!

It felt different than the others Tobias had bedded in the last few weeks. Even Angela who he enjoyed having sex with quite a bit, wasn't as intense as the desire that Tobias had for this Goth beauty turned momentary seductress.

The raven-haired young woman was a pale-skinned shadow that loomed over him for a moment, soon settling down on Tobias' alert and very stiff member, the young man jolting in surprise at how wet she had become.

"I can't help it, Tobias. You're doing something to me. I can't explain it!"

I can explain it just fine, Tobias thought, almost aloud, but was soon silenced with Cassidy's open mouth before he had a chance to respond.

I love this power! I love you, pill!

Tobias had his doubts about the power he had been given. But now, with Cassidy pressing her naked thighs against his own, her breathy moans of pleasure echoing in the old Dodge, Tobias forgot that he ever had a moment of doubt about it.

Episode Ten:

Superhero Syndrome

But it didn't stop there. There would be no morning after moment or waking up in an awkward state with someone that looks more like a stranger than a lover in the light like Tobias had become accustomed to with the pills.

The exploits in the car was simply that; a single exploit. They exchanged breath, fluids, moans, desire for one another. But neither Tobias nor Cassidy's thirst for the other were satiated by any means. If anything, this taste test made him desire her more.

"I'm taking you home with me so we can finish this."

As Cassidy put the car in drive and pulled out of the apartment complex, Tobias putting his jeans back on, his legs sore and arms aching from holding onto her for so long, sweat dripping down his back, neck, and other places that he needn't have to describe. But he couldn't keep his hands off her. Cassidy still hadn't dressed fully and, in moments, Tobias' fingers were inside of her, his other hand grabbing a handful of her hair between his fingers, his mouth on her neck and breasts that showed through the sheer black shirt that was sticking to her from their mingled sweat.

"What are you doing, Tobias? I'm trying to drive."

But Tobias' mind wasn't on anything but hearing Cassidy moan his name again.

"I can't keep my hands off you, Cassie."

He saw Cassidy blush a bit then, her eyes darting back to him every so often. Then, at a stop sign, she put the car in park and pressed Tobias' fingers further inside her.

"Oh my god, this feels so fucking good!" Cassie grabbed for Tobias' head and pulled him closer, their mouths hungry for one another, their hands having trouble deciding where to remain. A car stopped behind them, honked once, then passed them by slowly. But they didn't care any more.

*   *   *

The next morning, Tobias awoke with the brutal morning sun shooting through his shades, nearly as strong as Cyclop's optic blasts, Tobias using the corner of his pillow to guard against the morning that fully attacked him without warning.

My room? How did I get in my room?

Then his mind remembered the night with Cassidy and suddenly his left hand reached out for her on the other side of his bed. He found nothing but nothingness and sheets cold to the touch.

She's gone. Was it true? Did she stay the night? Did we go back to her place?

The young man took a deep breath in and could smell Cassie all over him, could taste her on his lips still, Tobias diving into the pillow to see if the smell breeched further than that.

He could smell eggs and sausage and coffee downstairs. Then his mom knocked on the door.

"Come in." His mother was dressed and ready for her morning workout.

"Tobias, honey, who was that pierced young lady that left early this morning?"

"Huh?"

"Is she your girlfriend?"

"I, umm, Mom. Can you not ask me about it right now? I'm still trying to process it myself."

"Oh, I see. You're her bitch then." Her mother said it so nonchalantly that Tobias had to take a moment to process what she had just said.

"What?"

"I've heard of these things on talk shows, dear. It's all right. Your father wasn't very assertive either."

"What are you talking about?"

"Tobias, honey, you're handcuffed to your bed."

"That stuff only happens in the movies. This isn't a movie!" But Tobias lifted himself up from his bed only to feel the cold pull of the handcuff on his right wrist, accompanied by the shackled echoed of the other side attached to his wooden bed frame.

"Well, if your life was a movie, what I heard through these walls last night would make it one of those trashy, late night movies that only pervs watch."

There was no comment or kind word that Tobias could come back with. He even had trouble looking his mother in the eyes as she sat down on his bed next to him, Tobias trying his best to hold onto his covers to cover as much of himself as possible, as he was sure he was completely naked underneath the sheets.

His mother spied the key to the handcuffs sitting on his bedside table and handed it to him.

"Thanks, mom."

She continued not to look at him, not in shame, but in embarrassment herself. Her face was a bit flustered and she had trouble keeping a straight face.

"You're welcome, Tobias. You know, I expect you to be a man. For a second, I thought you were going to come to me and tell me that you were gay or something."

"Mom! What? Are you crazy? I'm not gay!"

"And it would be alright if you were gay, sweetie, because I love you unconditionally. But you proved my theories wrong last night. Breakfast is ready for you downstairs. I'm going to go ahead and go to the gym. It looks like you've already had quite a workout."

Episode Eleven:

So it Begins

And the rest of the summer went something like this. Among frequent visits with Angela and Sadie, Tobias became well known with a woman. From the ashes of a dry, brittle under-sexed nerd came the sexual phoenix mythos, a young man coming into his own.

Soon, the convention was upon Tobias and his crew. Fan-Dome Comics and Collectibles had a regular booth and hotel reservations every year, bringing in most of their profit during the summer quarter in receipts from this convention in particular. And this was going to be Mark's first convention where he got to man the booth himself. Both his brother and father were traveling out of town to scope out another convention and he was getting full run of the booth with his friends as paid volunteers. After all, they were experts at all things comics.

In no time at all, the four of them were on the road, Mark and Junior in the U-Haul and Tobias and Clark in Tobias' mom's car for the weekend, heading off to destiny.

In a few hours, they arrived at the loading docks, Mark backing the U-Haul up in a loading bay for them to begin unloading. They were running a little late, so they got to unloading all of the product and table displays immediately, all four of them setting up and getting ready for the convention to open. Since it was just Thursday, preview night was only a few hours, from 4pm-9pm. Once they had the U-Haul emptied, Mark handed Tobias and Junior their hotel keys.

"Clark and I will take first shift here tonight and then Clark and Tobias tomorrow morning, with Clark and myself working in the afternoon and the next morning, with you and Junior working the next two days. The itinerary and schedules are in the packets you got earlier, so there shouldn't be any problems. Just get these keys activated at the front desk and make sure you pass out the flyers for the table at the pre-party."

"Pre-party?" Tobias looked clueless.

Marked nodded. "Yeah. You and Junior are tasked with going to the convention sponsor's pre-party. Everyone's going to be there. All you have to do is sit some of the flyers out for the table and give out some lobby cards on our deals. Should take you a few minutes at the most. We'll see you guys there once we close up here."

Once Tobias and Junior got checked in at the hotel and a fresh shower, it was nearly 6pm and the pre-party had already started.

At the sponsor's pre-party to really start everything off for the weekend, Junior and Tobias waited for Mark and Clark to finish setting up. The party was fairly busy and, after dropping off the lobby cards and flyers at any set of tables throughout the place, they were free to roam, which they did, getting their fill of some of the free food. It was there shift on the first day, so Tobias and Junior didn't expect to see them anytime soon.

Maybe in a few hours, Tobias thought. Already, Tobias had taken two pills and let them take effect, one of the scenarios on his list about to be checked off. Three cosplay women that they had seen come in earlier were next to Tobias, trying to get his attention.

Tobias had made it a point to walk by any attractive Catwoman cosplayer that he could find, keeping his distance from the rest of the women in the party if possible.

"Hey there." There was a slight nudge and Tobias turned to see a dark-skinned cosplayer dressed in a skin-tight Catwoman costume. Tobias smiled in response.

"Hey. How are you?" She answered him with a kiss on the cheek and a whisper in his ear.

"Better if you could get me out of this outfit." Tobias smiled against, accidentally making contact with Junior's virgin eyes, who looked on in utter shock and disbelief.

When Tobias went to the restroom to take a quick break from the party, Junior followed him in.

"What in the name of all that's holy is going on with you? Are you a pimp now? How are you getting these women? Better yet, where do I sign? Did you make a deal with the devil, cause I want in!"

Tobias tried to remain as calm as possible when answering, though his insides were exploding with excitement. After all, Tobias was still a nerd on the inside.

"I can't help you, Junior. I really can't."

He finished washing his hands and began to move away when Junior stopped him.

"Okay. I understand. It's some great secret. I get it. But you don't understand, Tobias. I'm a virgin. I've been a virgin all my life." He paused, looking around to see if there was anyone else in the bathroom.

"I'm going to college in a few weeks and I don't want to be the one without any experiences. I don't want to be the one that they laugh at. There, I've said my peace."

What could it hurt? How bad would it be to let Junior have a little fun? He's not out to hurt anyone. He wants to break the nerd ceiling that he's been living in for years, same as me.

"You have to do something for me, Junior." The look in Junior's eyes was one of desperation.

"Wait till we get back outside."

Junior looked over at the cosplay women rubbing on Tobias' shoulders, trying their best to lure him to the dance floor. He held them at bay for a few moments longer. Junior leaned over to Tobias.

"What is it? What do I need to do?"

"Go get a drink, a strong one, and bring it right back here." Tobias felt one of the women's hands on his thigh, steadily moving to the bulge in his pants that they had created from running their fingers through his hair.

He had always had a fantasy about cosplay Catwomen and now he was going to be able to act it out; with as many Catwomen as he wanted! He didn't know how, but he saw Junior getting a drink from the bar.

Junior was spitting and stuttering to the bartender the whole time, trying his best to seem adult, to be convincing. In reality, he was just eighteen, too. In the end, the bartender didn't even care; as long as the person getting the drink had an exhibitor badge around their neck it was fine. Tobias had to work quick. He slipped one of the pills he carried in his jean pocket into his mouth, biting it hard enough for the exterior pouch to break. He collected the nasty-tasting liquid in one cheek and waited for Junior to return.

This is some foul-tasting stuff, he thought decidedly, nearly gagging at its taste, never having tasted its contents, simply swallowing the pill down to let it do its work.

In another few seconds, Junior arrived and Tobias took the drink from him, spitting out the contents of the pill inside of it.

"Hey, I just bought that!"

He handed it back to Junior.

"Drink it! All of it!"

Junior watched as the glowing liquid mixed with the alcohol and lit up in his hand.

"What is this, Tobias? Some kind of witchcraft or something?"

"It's something that can make your wildest dreams come true, Junior. You want it or not?"

"Of course I do, Tobias! You know that!" Junior downed its contents, slamming the glass down on the table next to them. The girls cheered him on when Tobias began to.

"Alright, Junior. Let's have some fun!"

He hooked Junior's head in a mock headlock and took him out onto the dance floor with the women. The night began, a myriad of sweeping movements that took both young men to places only their imaginations could create. But for them, for one night, it was real. Everything was tangible; everything was at their fingertips.

And, for Junior, who had never had sex before, his virginity was about the have a field day.

*　　　　*　　　　*

Tobias lifted himself from the hotel bed the following morning, spying the several naked forms of women next to him. They were clustered here and there across the king size bed, one of them wearing Catwoman ears from a cosplay outfit; another ass was bared out for the world to see, the ass-bearing chaps keeping the dark brown cheeks well-defined and tight against one another, the young man trying his best not to wake them all as he got up. As he pulled his arm free from the fantastically assed mystery woman, he nearly tripped over a fully dressed cosplay Catwoman on the floor. She was fast asleep and lying on a pillow that had been taken from the king size bed. Even in the half-dark of the hotel room, Tobias could see the strong Asian features of her face.

She was oh so fun, Tobias suddenly remembered, looking down at the whip she held tightly in one of her gloved hands. *She was very naughty.* He tried his best to smile but then felt soreness in his jaw like no other.

Wonder what that was from?

The old Tobias would have jumped up in surprise at all of this ass, all of this pure, unadulterated woman around him at the moment, but then remembered that he was a well-practiced cocksman now and scratched his whiter-than-white ass through his Batman boxer shorts, heading to the kitchenette for a bottle of water.

Tobias returned shortly to the bed of women, a bottle of water in hand. He took a drink from it and sat it down on his nightstand, climbing back under the covers, crawling up over the naked limbs of one of the many sleeping women.

Just then, Tobias heard the bathroom door open and another woman, lightly stepping over the fourth Catwoman without waking her, climbing back into bed with the other two and himself.

Like all superheroes, I had to practice. I had to learn to use my powers; control them.

The unknown young woman next to him moaned slightly as Tobias pressed his face roughly down between her legs, waking her as well as her desire for him again. As he began working on her kitty parts, his jaw muscles tightened slightly, the soreness he experienced earlier coming alive but under control.

186

Oh, so that's what it was from, Tobias thought to himself, throwing one of Catwoman's legs up over his shoulder, her hands now guiding his mouth to his appointed destination.

This Catwoman, whomever she was, was in for a morning of practice.

Episode Twelve:

Trust Issues

It was Friday at the Illinois convention center and Tobias was on booth duty. He was set up at the corner of the comic boxes, giving prices, taking money, restocking from the bottom long boxes to the top, many times bringing entire long boxes up to replace the near-empty boxes on the tables at the booth. Both he and Clark had morning duty, so Tobias could feel the toll of the night before working on his energy levels. He smiled over at Clark, who walked over from the other side of the booth to him when it had finally slowed down.

"Junior can't stop smiling. He's got this goofy grin on his face this morning."

Tobias chuckled to himself.

Clark continued. "I saw him at breakfast this morning at the diner before we left. I didn't see you there. Busy?"

"Yeah, you could say that." Tobias' jaw was still sore from the thrashing he gave Catwoman this morning, her thighs nearly snapping his head off when she climaxed, waking the rest of those on the bed up with her noises. Tobias smiled at the thought of this and Clark must have caught the smirk on his friend's face, because he spoke up again.

"I heard a lot of noises last night. I went to investigate and found out it was your room. Know anything about that?"

Tobias continued to play dumb, but with a smile that gave it all away. "Don't have any idea about that.

Strange. Noises from my room? I wonder what that was?"

Clark was about to break his calm when the booth got busy again and he had to move back over to the other side of the booth to take customers. That's when Tobias noticed that Mark wasn't there. This was the first time getting to go on a convention trip in the place of his father.

Where is Mark, anyway?

"Hey, Clark, where is Mark at? Isn't he supposed to be here as acting manager?"

Clark nodded his head. "You're right there, sir! However, he told me he had pressing business with a female bounty hunter by the name of Captain Banda Pang. Said he was going to get her autograph, meet-and-greet or something like that. Said he would be gone for a couple of hours."

That's really not like Mark to skip on a chance to be at the booth in his father's place. And Banda

191

Pang, he said he didn't even like *Tracey Navens as an actress.*

Then something hit Tobias in the pit of his stomach. He knew not to get too upset at an insane theory; that was always something conspiracy theorists go crazy over. But Tobias had to check. He reached under the booth tables where all of their personal items were stored and grabbed his bag, pulling it out. He unzipped it, lifting all of the comics and signature pieces that he still had yet to get signed by the artists and writers and- *THEY WERE GONE!*

The bag of pills, the pills that he had used just last night, were completely gone. He looked around in the bag a bit, moving things here and there to see if he had put them in another part of the bag. He even unzipped the other compartments, looking in them to see if he had put them in there by mistake. But he had not misplaced them. He dropped the bag and grabbed a program as he left.

"I'll be right back, Clark."

"Hey, I can't man this place by myself!"

"Call Junior in then. I'm sure he'll take my place. We can trade out tomorrow."

"Everything okay?"

But Tobias didn't hear the concern in Clark's voice. He was already moving for the autograph area where Tracey Navens would be signing. He looked down at the program and skirted past some Weeping Angels cosplayers, looking for the signing times.

Yep, she should be signing now. All I have to do is get there and she should be there. I can warn her about-

But, as he approached her autograph signing area, he saw the long lines, weaving in and out of the dividing bars placed up for people to stand in line. And Mark was nowhere to be seen in the line.

He didn't have a VIP pass for her. Tobias went to the end of the line and tapped the last person on the shoulder, the Klingon cosplayer turning around.

"Yeah, what's up?"

"Shouldn't Tracey Navens be signing right now?"

"Yeah, she was here but then she had to leave. Someone gave her a message and she just got up and left the signing area. She didn't say anything about being back, from what I hear."

Mark Winterman! You're a dead man!

Tobias sped through the convention traffic back to the hotel, hoping beyond hope that it wasn't too late. *No telling how many pills Mark had taken.* And Tobias didn't know if there was such a thing as overdosing on them or not. Tracey Navens had no idea what she was getting herself into.

"Of all the people he could choose to use the pill on, why her? He knew that I liked-" Then it dawned

194

on him. *He's doing this out of spite, because I didn't share with him. He took all of my pills and the woman I have a crush on in the same, fatal swoop!*

Tobias hit the accelerator and zoomed onto the interstate, praying that it was not too late for his fantasy girl to be saved from Mark's depraved mind.

Tobias pulled up to the hotel, pulling into the parking lot just to the rear of the building, sprinting to the front lobby doors, past the attached diner straight to the front desk. With little effort because he was part of the company, he got a key to Mark's room and then moved through the lobby, straight to the elevators. He pressed the elevator button.

What the fuck am I going to do when I get up there? I'm no hero! He already knew that he couldn't fight, being eliminated by Mark's older brother earlier than summer.

Tobias had seen the moving truck that Mark used parked just outside, so he knew that he had made it back here. Whether or not he had a plan, Tobias watched as the elevator doors opened on their floor and nearly sprinted to Mark's room, sliding the card key. The green light came on to access the door and Tobias erupted through the door, seeing Mark half-naked and, upon further inspection, Tracey Navens in the process of naked. Her top was off and her breasts were exposed.

So that's what they look like! They were perfect in everyway. Which made it easier for Tobias to come at Mark swinging.

"This is what you do? This is it? You just steal from me and think I won't notice?" Tobias landed a punch and Mark jolted back in surprise, trying to pull up his pants from around his ankles.

"What are they, Tobias? You never told me! You never told any of us! I had to find out for myself."

Tobias saw the pills on the dresser; the bag of what his life had been made of the last few weeks.

"It's none of your business, Mark." Tobias swung at him again but missed this time.

"Stop trying to fight me, Tobes! I'm your friend."

Mark finally got hold of his pants and pulled them back up, reaching for the pill bag. He grabbed hold of it and moved for the window.

The window!

"No! Don't!" Tobias could feel his heart drop into his stomach as he saw Mark reach for the window lock and, before he knew it, saw Mark toss the bag out the window. Tobias went into a rage. He leapt at Mark and tackled him onto the floor.

"What gives you the right, huh? Who do you think you are?" Tobias slammed his fist into Mark's stomach, doubling him over. He cried out.

"I thought I was your friend."

"Friend? You never treated me like you're friend! I was your lackey, always doing things for you and listening to your shit!" Tobias was on him now, Mark covering his face from the attacks the angered nerd rained down upon him.

"I was never your friend because you were never my friend!"

In the scuffle and the heat of the moment, Tobias never noticed that Tracey Navens had called security, so he was a bit surprised when phantom hands appeared around him, pulling him off of Mark, his hands and feet still trying to strike out in any way possible.

Two security guards grabbed Tobias and escorted him out into the hallway until he calmed down, then into the elevator once he was calm enough to walk on his own. When the elevator doors opened up, Tobias could see straight out into the street to a hotel security vehicle's flashing lights. *I'm being directed into the vehicle, and possibly to jail!*

But Tobias never made it to the vehicle. As security was escorting him out, a voice stopped the two of the security guards in their place.

"Hey, that kid's with me. Bring him here." It was a bodiless voice at first until security escorted him further into the diner and he then saw who had spoken.

And the voice that spoke was someone that Tobias knew, too, which made it even stranger. There, sitting at a table at the diner connected to Tobias' hotel, was Vincent Gavano, one of the legendary comic creators of the first generation of comic writers and artists.

Episode Thirteen:

The Moment of Truth

Vincent Gavano, a man that every comic book geek looked up to in the industry, the old man that had nearly, single-handedly created the superhero industry with his comic creations. He was an old geezer by most accounts now, pock marks dotting his hands and face, both hands arthritic and slightly shaking as if he were excited about life and the things around him and Parkinson's had not set in as it had a few years back. And that's when he offered Tobias a seat in front of him.

To the crowd folk, Gavano always looked angry. Maybe it was just the expression on his face, as though he was forever taking an excruciatingly painful shit, or it was just the furrow in his brow, Tobias couldn't tell.

Either way, the old man was putting down some pancakes. There was an empty pancake-syrup riddled plate next to him and he was busy on another plateful.

The old man motioned to the security guards behind Tobias.

"You guys can let him go now. He was upstairs doing something for me. It was my fault. I should have gone myself. Then nothing would have happened."

The security guards stood there for a moment, dumbfounded.

"But we were told to escort him out of the building."

Vince looked around the diner attached to the ground floor of the hotel, trying his best to spy anyone else.

"I think you did your job, gentlemen. He's out of the hotel. Besides, he's no longer a threat to anyone, right? You won't have anymore trouble out of this kid here," pointing at Tobias with a forkful of pancakes, still dripping with syrup.

"Yes, sir, Mr. Gavano."

"Thank you, gentlemen." The two security guards left then, disappearing back into the hotel.

Vince took the bite of pancakes and then motioned to the seat in front of him with his butter knife.

"Have a seat."

"You're Vince Gavano, the creator of-"

"Quite a lot. I'm sure you've read some of my stuff at one point in time."

"Some? Oh my god, try almost all! All that I could get my hands on at the comic shop I go to."

"That's very flattering, son. Thank you, but I think we have more pressing things to speak of."

Just then, Tracey Navens walked by and Vince caught sight of her, waving a quick hello with yet another bite of pancakes.

"So, it was about her, huh? I can see why you would duke it out. She's one hot number."

"How do you know that? What, are you psychic?"

"No, I just have a penis and a brain, same as you. I know how the world works. I saw you come in a few minutes ago, shortly after your friend and Tracey."

"He's not my friend."

"I'm sure he's not." Vincent stuffed the forkful of pancakes in his mouth, chewing with delight.

"Shouldn't you be taking it easy? I mean, with your age and all?"

Vince took the bite and chewed it, all the while staring intently into the face of a still angry comic geek.

"Really, son? At this age, I'm trying to kill myself! Do you know how long I've been alive and what I've seen? No one needs to know the stuff that I know! That's why I stick to the small conventions now. I don't want to see anybody that I used to know. Remember, kid, my heyday years were the 1950's to the 1980's. After that, I didn't really give a shit anymore."

"So you've seen some pretty freaky shit?"

"More than my fill!"

"You ever seen one of your best friends getting a blowjob from your favorite celebrity?"

"Done it!"

"Have an older woman have sex in front of you in order for you to take notes on how to be a good lover?"

Without a beat, the old man continued to cut his pancakes.

"Done it!"

Tobias searched for another. He had a feeling this old man had had sex with multiple women dressed in superhero outfits at the same time already, so Tobias didn't even bother going there.

In fact, Vince may have created the characters out of his own fantasies.

"Well, have you ever dressed up in costume-"

"Come on kid! You really think I haven't-"

"Wait...Let me finish. Have you ever dressed in a superhero costume while your mother and her friends chase after you to fuck the shit out of you, all of this happening in public and on television?"

Vince nearly coughed on his mouthful of pancakes.

"That was you?" The old man sipped on some coffee to wash the pancakes down.

"Yep. Let's just say I have a way with women."

"But, your own mother?"

"No! Nothing happened. They just chased me but never caught me."

"Well, you got me beat there. I can't say I've had that happen to me. Say, how old are you, anyway? Twenty-one, twenty-two?"

"Eighteen."

"Jesus, kid! You trying to become a legend before your time or what?"

"Not really. Just making up for lost time. Well, at least lost time with the ladies."

"You must be a legend among your crew, huh?"

"Not really. Everyone kind of hates me right now. With the exception of a close friend."

"They're just jealous of you because of your luck with the ladies." Vince pointed with a fork loaded with a greasy bite of sausage and eggs at the hotel lobby.

"Was all that craziness one of your friends turned foes?"

"How did you know?"

"I had a lot of those in my time, believe me. If it wasn't over a woman, it was money; if it wasn't that, it was copyright of ideas. There was always a power struggle of some kind somewhere. You wouldn't have time in your young life to hear all of my stories of betrayal and woe."

The two sat that in Ruby's Diner in silence for a long moment. For the first time in some time, Tobias felt like somebody finally got him. For weeks now, he had been going through changes, transitioning into what he thought was an adult. But Tobias didn't feel anything like an adult.

And, if this is what being an adult felt like, I don't want to be one! The skinny, confused nerd didn't feel like he was ready for the world around him to suck full-time yet.

"It wasn't luck, Vince."

But Vince was in the midst of ordering another hot coffee and side order of pancakes. For a small guy, the old man could sure put away some food.

"What was that, kid?"

"It wasn't luck. I-"

"Prostitutes?" Done that, too."

"No, it's not that. Well, I don't think you'd believe me."

"Try me."

"I'm a superhero, Vince."

"You're shitting me with this, right? Is this one of those reality shows that dupe celebrities? Because, I have to tell you, Tobias, I don't like being on camera."

"No, this is real!" And that's when Tobias told the old comic artist and story creator his own story of debauchery and superheroism.

Four sausage links, a plate of pancakes, two pots of coffee, and a bathroom trip for the both of them, the story was finally told, out there in the open. Patrons had come and gone, the waiter had long since left them alone, unless they waved him down.

After Tobias finished his story, Vince was silent, his cold cup of coffee in his wrinkled hands as if it were still warm. As he tasted the coffee, he spit the cold beverage back into the cup and held it up above his head. In another moment, the waiter took his cup and brought it back full, along with another fresh pot in a warming canister for them both. It was a completely different waiter by this time, of course.

"Wow, Tobias. That's some story. You have a plan on what to do now? Besides go get that bag of pills back?"

The Pills! In sitting with the legend in front of him, he had forgotten completely about the pills and their possible whereabouts.

"I'll be right back."

Vince waved his cup of warm coffee at the young man as he dashed out of the diner and out the front door of the hotel as well, disappearing completely moments later.

Tobias looked up at the hotel from outside on the landscaped lawn and soon found where his hotel room balcony was, his eyes tracing the possible trajectory the pills could have followed in their downward descent after the skirmish with Mark. As soon as the young man's eyes made contact with the ground, his heart sank. Just outside his balcony window, the pool and a crowd of hotel patrons lay outside, many of them by the pool, some of them in it splashing around, while others were at the bar located inside the pool grounds, buying a drink to take poolside.

There's more than 50 people there now, Tobias groaned, making his way first to the outskirts of the pool area that was fenced in, hoping beyond hope that it fell straight down and landed in the well-manicured bushes just outside the pool area. After a few minutes of searching, Tobias turned up with a handful of nothing, now scanning the pool area without looking too suspicious. He took out his key card and scanned it at the entrance, walking into the pool area himself.

After 20 minutes of searching, Tobias came up with nothing. He looked up at the balconies just above him, his eyes squinting under the afternoon sunlight.

Maybe it fell onto another balcony, he thought, dreading the idea of the remaining pills being lost forever. *Wherever they may be, they're lost to me now.*

Tobias went back to the table where Vince had been and he was gone, the only thing left there was an empty set of dishes and two cups of cold coffee- and a card. Vince had left a business card half under Tobias' cup of coffee. Tobias picked it up and looked it over. He had never gotten a business card from a hero of his or from a celebrity as well as known as Vince was. And it had writing on it.

"'Enjoyed your story. It's not over. Call if you need an ear.'" Tobias pocketed it and went to salvage as much as he could of his final weekend with his friends.

Episode Fourteen:

Separation of Church and State of Mind

Tobias never made it back to the Fan-Dome table. Clark and the others intercepted him a few aisles away, right at the entrance to the convention, moving him to the side so they could talk to him. Clark had a look of concern on his face. The others did, too, but it was Clark who spoke first. He always seemed to be the voice of reason.

"I think it's best if you don't go back, Tobias."

But Clark hadn't just been referring to the Fan-Dome convention booth they had been manning the whole weekend. He meant the comic store, too. Forever.

"I can go back to the hotel and help you pack." Tobias accepted the offer gratefully. All of his other friends went back to the table. Even Junior, who Tobias had spent the previous night partying with, went back to the table after saying his goodbyes.

Tobias and Clark went back to get their things from the hotel, not saying much of anything, the situation still raw in Tobias' mind.

It had all come crashing down so quickly, so easily.

In just a few short weeks, Tobias' world had turned in upon itself. He had finally had good sex, been given some great gift that made women attracted to him, all the while ostracizing him from his friends of so many years. Once that started, he never thought in a million years that Mark- *well, I knew that he was willing to sell his own mother for a*

216

piece of ass, so why wouldn't this be any different? I had been something expendable to him. In the end-

He looked over at Clark, who was still packing up his things as well.

"Are you still my friend, Clark?"

Clark looked shocked that Tobias had said that.

"Of course I am, Tobias! You know I always hated Mark. It was about time someone put him in his place. Too bad I wasn't there to see it. He's just like his brother, that Mark. Always thinking about himself and no one else. They may not look alike but they're one and the same when it comes down to it."

The ride home in the car wasn't sad and as depressing as Tobias thought it would be. They put their bags in the trunk, drove for about 100 miles, then stopped to get something to eat at a small diner just off the nearby exit.

"What was it like," Clark asked, digging into his meatloaf plate, cutting the loaf into smaller pieces so he could dip them in the small serving bowl of gravy that had been placed on the side.

"What was what like, Clark? You're going to have to be more specific than that." Tobias could tell that his friend was teasing a bit, but he got to the point after he took a few bites of his food.

"Beating up the two brothers that everyone else would have died to beat up. It's no fair, you get to have all the fun."

Tobias knew that he had not even come close to "beating up" Douglas, but he did do quite a number on Mark, still feeling the sting that the soreness brought in his knuckles when trying to hold his fork to eat his own plate of meatloaf, mashed potatoes, and corn.

"I don't know. I haven't really had a chance to process it yet. I guess you're right though, Clark. Everyone else did want to beat them up."

"'You're my hero, Tobias.'" Clark's best damsel in distress voice always worked for making others laugh, which it did, Tobias having to cover his mouth with a napkin so as not to spit out his food.

"And I totally saw her tits. In their full glory." Clark nearly dropped his fork in surprise.

"You're kidding me, right?"

"No. They happened to be out when I came into the room."

"And? Don't leave me in suspense, man!"

Tobias just smiled. "They were so perfect! Like Halle Berry in Swordfish perfect."

Clark's face flushed in excitement.

"Tell me all the details, Tobias Merchon. That's the least you can do for the lunch I'm about to buy you!"

*   *   *

It was just as Clark had said it was going to be. A few days later, Clark brought Tobias the rest of his hold box from the comic store and said that his box had been cancelled by the powers that be and that Tobias was no longer welcome in the store. Mark had somehow made Clark the messenger for his evil deeds. But Clark didn't mind, not in the least. He had emptied his own hold box and walked out of the store, never looking back as he did so.

He did it for friendship, Clark later told Tobias, clapping him on the back as he left for college the following week, Indianapolis bound on a Greyhound, Clark saying his final goodbyes a few days before leaving.

His future was suddenly upon him and now Tobias was running out of time the last few days of summer.

He had said his goodbyes to Ms. Angela, the young man still feeling her urging hips on him as she gave him a final goodbye in her bed, both of them lighting up this time. Tobias didn't know when he'd be seeing her next.

But that was the best goodbye gift anyone had given me.

Tobias looked at the last of the boxes he had boxed up in his room, looking for the first time in years at the room as it had been before he had occupied it: empty, naked walls, no longer covered in comic book posters and print outs of famous blog posts he had commented on. No longer were there stacks of graphic novels alphabetized on the bookshelf in the corner of his room or the statues he had been paid in for doing inventory at Fan-Dome all those years ago.

Even the sets of action figures, both carded and loose, had been packed up, the boxes stacked in the corner of the room now, waiting to be put into a storage facility while he was away.

And my comics. The nine long boxes in the corner had connected him to the world of a number of heroes and villains and helped him to get his scholarship he was about to collect on in the next few days, taking his first step in graphic arts and storyboard art, his own destiny being made simply because of his love of comics and the stories behind them. He had taken out a few of his favorites and put them in a short box to take with him.

The short box as well as a stack of other boxes, his backpack with his laptop in it and his luggage, was all placed by the front door and ready to be loaded into the car.

But I won't be here much longer any way. Off to college and stuff. Stuff. That's a good one. I wonder what good I'll be now that I don't have anymore pills.

Tobias had no idea what he was going to do now that he was no longer the stud of old. He had no luck in retrieving what was left of the pills after the skirmish with Mark.   The bag was nowhere to be found.

But it wasn't exactly like I could ask anyone about its whereabouts, Tobias decided, knowing that the existence of the pills themselves would be in question if anyone did find them and connect Tobias to their origins.

I guess it's for the best, Tobias concluded, looking through his phone from time to time at the scores of women that he had been with, probably none of them even willing to approach him without the pill in full effect. *It was good while it lasted.*

Goodbye, Bolingbrook.   Goodbye, Fan-Dome. Goodbye, secret identity. Goodbye, pills and the life that came with it.   Tobias guessed he would never find out who gave him the pills. It was time to move on and be normal Tobias Merchon the comic nerd.

Episode Fifteen:

Countdown to College

Stratton University was just on the outskirts of Springfield, Illinois, located 180 miles south of Bolingbrook. It took Tobias close to three hours to get there in the Merchon-Mobile with his mom. The Mazda was packed to the rim; the trunk, the back seats, as well as a few bags of things in the passenger seat in his lap.

No sooner had his mother drove onto the campus with him and dropped him off than his phone vibrated. It was his mother. She hadn't left the campus more than three minutes.

MOM: YOU GET THERE OKAY, SON?

<u>**TOBIAS**</u>: YOU JUST DROPPED ME OFF, MOM. I'M FINE.

<u>**MOM**</u>: DID YOU PACK TOILET PAPER? I CAN SEND YOU SOME IF YOU DIDN'T.

<u>**TOBIAS**</u>: SEND ME SOME? THEY HAVE TOILET PAPER HERE, MOM. I GOT THIS.

<u>**MOM**</u>: AND CONDOMS. DID YOU GET THOSE?

<u>**TOBIAS**</u>: MOM!

<u>**MOM**</u>: OKAY, SON. CALL ME IF YOU NEED ME.

*   *   *

Financial aid, paperwork, college apartment with a roomie, getting groceries for the first time without thinking about his mother's favorite foods. *Seeing pretty geek girls pass by and saying nothing.*

Somehow, Tobias' mojo no longer responded to women anymore. It was as if-

-the pill made me who I was then. That I no longer existed as anything but what I was before this

226

whole experience. I wonder if other superheroes had this trouble. But, right away, Tobias knew the answer.

Guy Gardner, for starters. From the beginning, the character Guy had known that he was destined for greatness and, though he was an asshole throughout most of the history of his character, he always felt that he should be the ring bearer for Sector 2814. Even when Hal Jordan walked away from the responsibilities and Jon Stewart took over, Guy Gardner was there vying for the place.

I guess this is my place. Tobias looked around at the campus now. It was filled with several sets of small buildings clustered together, a maze-work of sidewalks connecting each smaller courtyard to one another until it all expanded around the Main Building.

It was a four-story building called the Bennett Building, named after a professor that had attended years ago, but Tobias had another name for it: The

Baxter building. It looked nothing like where the Fantastic Four resided in the comics, Tobias remembering well a skyscraper that shot high into the sky, *but it's the biggest building on campus.*

Tobias was swamped with college work and projects for his classes within the first few weeks. Besides the first set of storyboards for a mock film, Tobias had an English paper and Geometry study sheets that beyond baffled him.

I can do this, Tobias reminded himself. *I came here for a reason. The workload and the difficulty of this semester acclimatizing from high school to university will not deter me!*

The young college student was in Mapping the Human Mind class now with Professor Stanley and nearly 75 other students, the white-haired old man looking like a reincarnation of Johnny Knoxville's Bad Grandpa.

228

He even wore cardigans sweaters over dress shirts, Tobias noticed. The old man was in full swing with his lecture today.

"Now, the idea of looking into the mind and mapping it out is not new, oh no. In the Dark Ages, there were a few that believed that there were parts of the brain that controlled thoughts, movements even the animal-like side of man. But, of course this couldn't be proved until centuries later when-"

And the class went on like this for another 45 minutes, Tobias taking a copious amount of notes.

Tobias had no idea that someone was watching him though. Since the beginning of class, they had been watching him. And now, when the moment was right, they made their presence known. Tobias felt a tap on the shoulder. He turned.

"Hi, Tobias." It was Goth chick- Cassidy- but it wasn't really. It was another incarnation of her. Instead of the Goth chick that he had known, there was a polished conformist in front of him, staring back with a smile that contained no piercings. She wore a small black blouse that complimented her figure and a matching black business skirt. She even had earrings that didn't have skulls on them.

Tobias smiled back, at a loss for words. Well, except these.

"Cassidy, I- Um, how did you get here? Are you-"

"-going to this university? Nah. I've got a college that I go to already. But you wouldn't know that, now would you? We never talked about things."

She was quiet enough not to disturb Professor Stanley's present rant. Tobias kept his eyes on her, still amazed to see her in his class.

"You're right. We never got a chance to talk. About things."

"And stuff."

"Yeah, and stuff." Tobias almost felt bad, like he had taken advantage of her.

230

"And this." Cassidy sat something down on the table in front of him. It was small, almost completely clear, but the glow was unmistakable.

A pill! But-

"How did I know? Well, someone had to give them to you, right Tobias?"

"You gave them to me?"

"Actually, out of pity, I was trying to give them to Mark that night so he could get a life. But you were-"

"-wearing his poncho! Mother fucker!" That last word came out a bit louder than he'd have liked it to, half of the class turning around, including the professor, who was trying to figure out who Cassidy was. His professor spoke up.

"I'm sorry, miss, but are you enrolled in my class?"

"No, I'm not, sir. I was just leaving."

Cassidy smiled at Tobias and got up to leave.

"I'll be waiting outside to talk about stuff when you're done."

And then she was gone, the pill left slightly glowing on the table in front of him. The class returned to their upright positions and Professor Stanley's voice retained the familiar boringness that it had before, not missing a beat.

Tobias had trouble keeping down his lunch. *Cassidy, the whole time? She was the giver of the pill? But why?*

Tobias grabbed up his things, slipping the pill into his pocket, practically shooting through the door to find her.

Maybe the end wasn't the end after all. Maybe that end was just the beginning.

For what, Tobias did not know, but he was willing to find out where it would take him.

THE END

Epilogue

The interrogation room was dimly lit when the cop came out of it, the sobs by the suspect heard throughout the back room until the door shut and sealed out the sound. The detective looked at the perp in the room, shaking his head.

"How the fuck did he do it? That's all I want to know. Is he some kind of genius or something?"

The defense attorney shrugged his shoulders.

"I wish I could tell you. He says that he wasn't doing anything that day in the hotel. That, and I quote, 'I was just swimming and hanging out with my friends and we were about to go to the convention when I found them.' End quote."

"You've got to be fucking kidding me! You mean to tell me that he finds some drugs, shares them with his friends, and then there's an all out orgy at the pool until the police break it up and he's playing innocent?"

The detective bit his lip.

"That kid is going to break and tell me who gave him this." He lifted the evidence bag full of blue, shiny pills, each one of them glowing independently of one another.

"Oh, he's going to tell me. And we're going to bust these clowns!"

AUTHOR'S NOTES

I had a single image, a single scene that defined what this novel (now novel series) was going to be in April of 2012. The moment that I had it, I called a friend and told him. He said, well, what anybody who doesn't know what the fuck you're talking about. 'What the fuck are you talking about?' At that time, I had already started three different novel series and this book didn't seem to fit into any of them. Hence the creation of THE YOUNG GENTLEMAN'S NOVEL!

I didn't want to be writing for two demographics with my erotic fiction series so the new series took shape for those that were younger and didn't deal with marriages or complex relationships yet. I wanted those that were just beginning to dabble in sex, scared of the idea of it, or had broken through their adulthood and still had yet to, to take heart that they weren't alone.

From what I've seen out there, there are not many erotic fiction stories that speak for the common man/woman. I personally get tired of writing about the well-defined man with a perfect job that stumbles across a series of picture perfect sexual encounters that many would die for if they had the chance to experience. And The Pill was born.

About the Author

Little is known about the author, TITUS STRONG. Taking his name from a classic Shakespearean dramatic hero, the author writes stories that fill the imagination with lust and humor, all the while waiting for his own next sexual conquest, forever filling his time with fantasies that wait to be fulfilled themselves.

Coming Soon From TITUS STRONG:

- ♥ How Santa Ate My Cookies and other Festive Tales of Erotic Fiction
- ♥ A Corporate Feeling: Book Two of a Man's Romance Novel
- ♥ The Pill: Second Dose

www.ingramcontent.com/pod-product-compliance
Lightning Source LLC
Chambersburg PA
CBHW061033120726
47910CB00006B/2232